THE ONE
FROM THE
STARS

THE ONE FROM THE STARS

KESHAV ANEEL

Srishti
PUBLISHERS & DISTRIBUTORS

SRISHTI PUBLISHERS & DISTRIBUTORS
Registered Office: N-16, C.R. Park
New Delhi – 110 019
Corporate Office: 212A, Peacock Lane
Shahpur Jat, New Delhi – 110 049
editorial@srishtipublishers.com

First published by
Srishti Publishers & Distributors in 2017

10 9 8 7 6 5 4 3 2 1

For every child from a middle class family,
who had to quit on his dreams
due to lack of money.

Acknowledgments

I can never thank you enough Merril Di for being an amazing support system. My journey could never have been this smooth without you. I hope I will have you forever to read my first drafts and design every single thing for my books.

Ryan, Paras, Vishal, Gaggi, Himanshu – you guys are the most dedicated artists and filmmakers I have ever come across. The hard work you all have put in was sensational. Your love for your work is amazing and pure. Thank you for the trailer. It's a privilege to be a part of your team. I am sure I am in for a great learning curve.

Also, Rubby, Dharminder sir and Renu ma'am – thank you for turning up at such a short notice. Being great theatre artists, it was modest of you to have cooperated in every possible way. Certainly, we shall do many more projects together. Knowing all of you was a complete honour.

Likhit Avasthi – my pal for life – I owe you big time for the two beautiful poems that you allowed me to use in this book. Trust me, nothing else could have suited my requirement more than yours sweetly written couplets.

Sparsh, Tushar, Paarth, Pujeet, Bhuvan – my most treasured school time friends – I love you guys, and I don't think I'd ever be able to describe in words what your support means to me.

Amit, Sanchit, Keshav Sethi, Jaffy, Ashish, Madhav, Navpreet, Rupinder – my MBA friends – I have never met so many wonderful souls under one roof at a given point of time. You guys inspired this book to happen, and I can never forget the faith you always showed in my ability. My life wouldn't have been full of sweet memories had you not been such an integral part of it.

Pankaj, Ashima, Romila, Pooja, Surbhi, Himanshu, Pushpak, Abhilasha, Yashika, Raghav Uppal, Farhaaz, Jagjeet, Ajay Ohri sir, Anil sir, Nikhil, Shubham, Aditya, Dhwani – thank you guys for bearing with me and supporting me through thick and thin. We met somewhere in the middle of life and what an absolute treat it has been knowing all of you. You guys are my bright stars, my coolest friends, and the people I can blindly trust.

Team Srishti – Jayanta Da, Arup Da, Stuti and everyone behind the scenes – thank you for being kind and understanding.

Last, but not the least, my readers – for all the support, encouragement, reviews (both positive and negative), and faith in my work – thank you. I will continue to write for all of you. There is no Keshav Aneel without your love and acceptance.

Prologue

I HAVEN'T BEEN ABLE TO SLEEP SINCE LAST NIGHT. NOW ALSO, when I am sitting on my bed with legs folded, trying to feel at ease by taking deep breaths like Yogi Baba speedily does like a tractor's engine, this anxiety is killing me!

"What should I do?" I scratch my head, thinking hard. It is hot outside, and even if I ignore that for a while and go out, it won't be of any use. All my friends are already out watching a movie.

Maybe I should have accompanied them when they asked. Anyhow, no use repenting now.

The next few minutes, I try to keep myself busy, irritably staring at the fan over my head, which, by the way has descended down directly from the 1970s, oscillating so slowly as if begging me to show mercy.

"Papa should throw you out of the house," I mutter at it. "Can't produce one percent air of the noise you do." But

I cannot request Papa to dispose it off. After all, it is the last memory of my grandmother Smt. Pepsi Devi. She gifted it to Grandpapa on his first birthday after marriage. Maybe to make love comfortably during the scorching heat of summers.

Then, as my eyes suddenly fall on the cuckoo clock, I thunderously stretch to my left and pick up the television remote from the bedside. Pressing the power button, I straightaway tune in to my favourite show: *Master-Chef India*. Though I had watched this episode the previous evening too, I won't mind repeating, even if it was for the millionth time. Basically, the sight of sumptuous meals and the dimpled smile of the handsome judge-chef is certainly an irresistible combo.

To my disappointment, an advertisement is running; a women empowerment ad to sell shorts. A new way of fooling us customers when they don't intend anything beyond sales.

I flip through channels and throw away the remote in frustration. Daily soaps aren't my cup of tea and news channels have become so annoying these days that one feels there is nothing positive going on in the world. I pull my phone out of my pocket and refresh the 'results' page of the CBSE website.

Hopefully, they have taken pain to update something.

Chandigarh Zone Class XII Results to be announced tomorrow at 08:00 hrs, it reads.

My eyes widen.
Holy Cow! They have finally declared the date!
I zoom in, giving it a closer look and dash to Mumma, shouting.

"It'll be out tomorrow, Mumma. They will be posting it tomorrow…Where are you?"

She isn't in her room. Washroom, maybe.

And as I am about to knock on the door, she opens it, wiping her hands with a white towel. She drops it over her shoulder, hurrying to hold my phone and confirming it for herself. Taking it in her hands, which are still a little wet, she checks the announcement and looks at me with hope.

"This should be good, beta. We have a lot of expectations from you." She has this serene smile on her face while saying this, but I cannot even imagine what hopes hide behind it.

"Don't know, Mumma, but I've—"

I am cut short by the sound of a familiar car horn. It's close to the gate.

"Is it Papa?" I ask taken aback.

"I think so," she says, and walks to the window quickly. "But what's he doing here in the afternoon?"

"How would I know? He didn't call or message me either," I reply in an undertone.

"Oh yeah, it's him darling." She half turns, dropping the curtain. "Help him out."

Papa brings the car in. We exchange a smile, and as it passes, I close the gate and run to him. Mom comes out too.

The engine stops, and as I hear the sound of the car unlocking, I open the right back door to pick up his bag, tiffin and everything else.

"You didn't tell me you were coming early, Dhruv," Mom says.

"Had a severe headache. Moreover, there weren't many customers as it's a Monday today."

"Should I get you a Disprin, Papa?"

"No allopathic stuff," he says, gently pushing the door and putting the keys into his pocket.

I walk inside following my parents. Keeping the lunch box on the slab in the kitchen, I get a glass of water for Papa. He drinks it in one go.

"Would you like some cold coffee?" Mom asks.

"With some extra sugar," he replies, nodding quite aggressively, which only goes on to show how disturbing the headache is. He hands over the glass to me and bends to untie his shoe laces.

"For me too, Mumma," I say as Mom collects the empty glass from me, and prepares to leaves.

"It's tomorrow," I say nervously.

"What?" Papa asks casually, pointing towards the AC switch.

"My…umm…bo…board results," I reply, turning the air-conditioner on.

"Don't fret," he answers, kicking his right shoe beneath the bed. "In case you fail, you may appear for the exams next year, no worries," he adds.

"What are you saying Papa?" I grunt very harshly.

He laughs.

I stare at him in anger, almost on the verge of saying, "Had you not been my father, I would have punished you justly for those words."

"Come here!" He reaches out to hold my hand, making me sit next to him.

I am freaking agitated. A dreadful thought runs in my head, *"What if goddess Saraswati was sitting on his tongue? His words will become true and my whole life will be spoiled."*

"Listen, beta. Marks don't carry any value. Stop bothering about them. They won't assure you of a smooth road in life. More significantly, forty people under one roof can never be equally good at doing the same thing. So making a judgment on the basis of what you call a report card, with exact same parameters for all, when each one is so clearly different, is absolutely stupid."

"But Papa, all my friends, Usha Aunty, Narayan Uncle, our relatives, they are all waiting, and it will be so insulting if anything goes wrong," I finally let it out.

"Nothing shall go wrong, my child," Papa replies. "But the fear I see on your face, this is what worries me actually."

"Fear?" I am a bit amazed. *"Why would that worry him? I mean, isn't it supposed to be natural in an eighteen-year-old girl?"*

"Do you know where this comes from?" Papa asks.

"Failing to live up to your expectations?" I make a guess.

"No, absolutely not!" he says immediately.

"Then what?" I ask

"You tell me." He gives me another chance

"Umm…Your scolding me?" I say, thinking hard.

"Has that ever happened?" He is surprised by my answer.

"Oh yeah! That can't be… Sorry…Then what?" I ponder hard, but in vain.

Papa seems to be enjoying my confusion. He has his eyes fixed on me, and his grin indicates that he is sure I am not coming up with an answer. I give up, feeling discouraged.

"You tell me," I innocently request.

"Alright!" he says. Taking a deep breath, he speaks up, "This state of mind, this fear, this anxiousness which you presently have, is actually the side effect of not knowing your true purpose, my child."

"Umm…as in?" I ask

"Look, when you are sure how *you* want to see yourself by the end of your time – which by the way is too limited to be doing what you don't love – you are bound to get so obsessed that appreciation and criticism will hardly have anything to do with your efforts."

"Is it that easy to not waver on the path of one's inner calling?" I question.

"To be honest, you have to have someone supporting you. Be it your own destiny, or a person close to you, like one of your parents maybe, or your spouse, or any best friend. Without it, adversity can get the better of you. Because fighting alone for a cause, with no one around to hold you, motivate you, teach you, can actually break you into pieces….No person is an island, you see."

"Hmm. That sounds deep. Can you tell me a bit more about it, Papa? I mean, how a human being gets success, what are the common reasons of failing? Why certain people do better than the even those with much more capability and IQ? I really want to know your thoughts on this."

"Well, there can be an event or a period in your life that positively shakes you up, or something may happen that takes you to the right place at the right time. But then, yes, there are exceptions who have defied this school of thought. There have been several people in history who fought against the tide of time and came out with flying colours."

"Suppose I fail following my heart, what would your reaction be?"

"If you happen to lose something that would stop you from growing old, prevent you from falling sick, or let slip away something that could have given you supernatural powers, making you immortal like StarFire or a Zatanna, I would certainly feel bad for you. Otherwise, it's all a part of the learning process, I would say," Papa says, very evenly.

I am amazed by his answer. What a stable and a calm head he has got!

"Not every parent thinks this way. Not all of them are so supportive and understanding like you, Papa. I wonder at times when all of my friends' parents keep cribbing about marks and outcomes and everything, you encourage me to give my best shot at whatever I feel happy doing. That's my good fortune, don't you think?" I say proudly and lovingly.

"I am happy you value it, my child." He pats my back.

"But trust me, I can never be half as good a parent as you. I mean, it's sometimes impossible to ignore society, their never-ending questions and everything that constantly revolves around sucking the peace out of one's mind. I wonder how you manage to do it."

"Always remember this, Somaya: Whenever you find a maturity that dazzles you, a sense of responsibility and frankness that you can only wish to incorporate in yourself, know that the suffering has been the most there, and the lessons have been the hardest."

"I didn't understand what you just said."

He looks at the floor, shaking his head. "Nothing," he answers after a while. "I will explain it to you some other day."

"No, Dhruv. I think it's the right time for her to understand," Mumma interrupts. She has been standing behind us, listening. "It's her time to choose a path, and I think his life will not only be a great book of guidance for her, but she will also come out to be an improved human being."

"Hmm…maybe," Papa mumbles, lost in thought.

Who is this 'he' they are talking of, I wonder.

"Well, in that case…Why are you standing there? Come over here and help me out," Papa asks Mumma.

"Alright, let me get the cold coffee and something to eat," she says, returning with a tray in her hand that carries three brown glasses of coffee.

I jump out to help. I hold the tray while she pulls out a small plastic table from the bedside to be kept on the bed. She then grabs a pack of cookies and some snacks from the kitchen, after which the three of us settle on the bed with our glasses.

Papa takes a sip and sighs. He keeps the cup on the headboard, rubs his hands, and begins...

I CAN VIVIDLY RECALL THE LAST FEW MINUTES OF THE LAST class of our management course. It had turned out to be a near-perfect session with Professor Swami. He had shared with us that day some very powerful insights like: "Dharma is not in following Hinduism or Islam or Christianity; it's daring to set on a voyage where you determine the hidden ability within, and that discovery is your individual key to the path of eternal happiness."

For the entire lecture that day, he preferred simplifying life to us, sharing similar quotes of discovery, spirituality, self-attainment and all that could possibly help motivate a fresh young soul. The class throughout the hour maintained a rare silence with zero interruption. Honestly, not everyone was listening to him carefully; most of them were sleeping with their eyes open, except for one – Vishesh Raghav, my best friend. He was an avid dreamer who loved to talk of making it big in life, and though he was quite an ordinary fellow in studies, he was someone very extraordinary on stage.

I knew him since school days and had never heard him losing any debate, elocution, extempore or poetry recitation competition. He seemed to be on some elixir each time he participated and was an extraordinary playwright and actor, having single-handedly won innumerable plays and mock parliamentary debates for the university.

All in all, one could say, in a good for nothing batch, where half of the people had plans to go to Canada and most others eyed their family business, fully aware that no company would mistakenly hire them, my best friend was a complete misfit. Usually, someone of Vishesh's calibre, taste and quality should logically have been in the National School of Drama or Whistling Woods, or doing something in creative writing in an American University. But in India, you find such people either preparing for bank exams or working in a multinational company.

Nonetheless, Vishesh was going to fight for his dreams unlike many others. He, for us, was already a superstar, and we could bet that it was just going to be a matter of some more time when the world too would agree.

Vishesh Raghav oozed this magical attitude of never giving up, and one unforgettable testimony to his character which echoes in my ears even today was the poem that he had recited after our ceremonial farewell speech. It was like sharing with us an ever eternal promise that he had made to himself on which he would never back down.

THE ONE FROM THE STARS

I have picked up the pieces,
Now just putting them together,
Neither good times stay nor bad ones,
But this attitude stays forever.

Gasping breath weak body,
The stride is still way too long
The luck is fake, the failure namesake,
The will is tough, the spirit strong
You have an opinion, I respect it,
You will honour mine, I suspect it.

I can join your party
If I am rich, powerful and clean
Won't get the gate pass
Because the high is always a bit mean.

The path was my choice
I will keep walking the road
None will motivate me better
So criticize, judge and goad.

The world fears and warns,
Everything that is uncertain and hazy
Alas, you won't believe till I do it…
Till then just call me crazy.

And he signed off from the stage, modestly signalling a thumbs-up as we stood clapping with a hunch that this boy who leaves people mesmerised every time, will make it big very soon. Enthralled as we were by the charm of his polite yet emphatic voice, we all settled down for the last act. They then played clips of our moments in the university along with Corey Tynan's 'Hold on to the memories...' in the background. Within no time, most people inside the auditorium (even our juniors) were in tears.

We were helplessly watching the sun setting down on the golden days of our lives and we could do nothing. The photographs were making us emotional. They were going to remain in our hearts forever, but there were sadly going to be no more late night studies, no more canteen *ki chai*, no more roaming inside the department corridor, no more road trips and no more of life in life, to be honest. It seemed that the beautiful journey of two years had come to an end within a few seconds.

We gathered outside for some more pictures, before finally leaving, running to each other to not miss out on a souvenir. Selfies, hugs, promises, giggles, jokes and every other emotion came purely from deep within. Then, as the clock struck 1800 hours, the security guards jumped in whistling, instructing particularly the girls to leave for their rooms or PG accommodations or their houses.

Everyone slowly set off with heavy hearts, leaving behind the most beautiful part of themselves. A few had trains to catch, a few were going to stay back in the hostel for a day or two, while a few like us were locals. I waited for my group in the parking. Vishesh, Jaffy and Pujeet came walking together with coats hung over their shoulders and shirt-sleeves rolled up. The four of us exchanged a look, smiling from the corner of our mouths, giving a 'let's pretend nothing will ever change' look. It didn't help us a bit from the inside though, as Pujeet had a flight soon after. He was about to leave for Toronto forever.

Making one honest confession here: the moment we got to know about his future plans, we right away wanted to snatch his passport and tear it up, ordering him to dare not ever leave us. But for the sake of his career, that being explicitly significant for material gains and also being a crucial factor in deciding societal reputation, none of us could gather the courage to revolt.

We, with long faces, got inside the Innova, and then just as I pressed the gas, Vishesh's phone rang.

"Ram Lal?" Jaffy guessed, moving his neck like a cobra to figure out the caller.

Vishesh snapped to his right and kicked him with full force. "My father's name is Sri Hari Lal Raghav, alright? Say it with respect the next time."

We cackled as Jaffy, holding his knee, yelped like a wounded puppy.

"Imbecile!" Vishesh muttered.

"Buddy, your phone is ringing." I brought his attention back, looking at him in the rear-view mirror.

It was our junior Nishtha on the other side, his girlfriend, insisting on seeing him once again. We weren't letting him go, because what drama on earth was that! Both these love birds had spent the whole day together and now again they wanted to meet. But then Vishesh pleaded, we melted and the lovers won. Nevertheless, a clear instruction to him was to meet us outside the main gate in ten minutes or he could return home getting crushed in a tempo.

"He won't come back thirsty anymore," Jaffy commented, watching his back.

"Why is your mind always in a gutter?" I slammed.

"Because all my friends live there," Jaffy replied

"Yesterday I was reading the newspaper," I said, "and an advertisement regarding a job opening reminded me of you, Jaffy."

"Aha! What's the package they are offering, brother?" he asked, suddenly getting very serious.

"Listen to the details first."

"Yeah, please," Jaffy said.

"That the Japanese porn industry…is in dire need of men. They only have eighty male performers against five thousand female porn stars. So I was wondering why you don't go and join. Send a few bare pictures of your sexy golden-brown body standing in front of the mirror. I am sure they'll be impressed."

Pujeet chuckled. "Great idea, man! Then your sex story, oh sorry, I mean, success story will be world over, and your parents will be so proud of you."

"You first tell me this, nigga," Jaffy said, "Why the fuck did the ad remind you only of me?"

Pujeet and I looked at each other and broke into laughter. The offended Jaffy switched to the middle of the back seat, pressing our necks, groaning. "Who do you think I am? A whore, huh?"

To pass time till Vishesh came, I drove the car for a university tour. It was our everyday habit to drive around together in the morning, during the lunch break and then before returning home in the evening, never missing out on it even during exam days. It was like an intense addiction to us and that was altogether a different taste of fun. That being said, like all good things, this too was the end of it.

The three of us looked outside, recalling our unforgettable days here. We talked about what it was like walking around for the first time as a fresher and falling in love with the place, celebrating in the rain, hurriedly racing off to class, randomly pressing the fire alarm for fun, hooting for no reason, intentionally wearing similar superman T-shirts to grab girls' attention and what not!

Completing two rounds, we reached close to the gate and Vishesh appeared within a minute. I instructed everyone to change and be ready, and I would pick them up at around 8 p.m. as we had to drop Pujeet at ISBT-43, from where he was going to Delhi to spend the next day with his cousin before flying away.

Vishesh immediately regretted that he wouldn't be able to join. He had already gone against his family's wishes and not taken up any placement, and then, despite being instructed to not attend the farewell, he had. So now if he were to seek permission to go out again, his father would surely kill him.

We did understand his situation as Hari Lal Uncle was very short tempered, but these were the last few hours of us together. The three of us begged him to join us somehow. Vishesh showed his helplessness as he'd have to face his angry dad back home. He could take that for one day for us, we requested with folded hands. Knowing that he would be scolded badly, he still agreed for our sake, asking us not to come to his house and rather wait for him in the Sector 26 market.

Poor him! He was going to lie. He had no other option. And why? Because he had overtly conservative parents who were quite desperate to see him in a job that assured security, safety and money. On the other hand, my friend was completely a rebel and had clear intentions to follow his heart. Due to this, the Raghavs kept Vishesh under a strong check, stopping him from doing anything that would distract his attention.

True that Vishesh came from a middle class family and had much more to lose than anyone else, but why bar him from flying in the sky? Why not let him be who he was? Why try to make him toe the line and become a copy of someone else?

From his maternal uncle to the most distant uncle's uncle, everybody explained to Vishesh that his vision was childish and nobody ever gave him a single chance to justify the rationality of the journey he wanted to embark on. Uselessly, in order to prove themselves and their wisdom right, they declared Vishesh disrespectful, egoistic, selfish, worthless, and everything that he wasn't.

I felt bad for my friend. Why was it that his first fight was against the ones supposed to love and support him the most? Why did the people, who by being on his side could have given him an unparalleled strength, chose to consider him foolish and discourage him instead?

Unfortunately, no one fathoms the intensity of adversity on paths where the probability of success is already very low. In place of offering courage to such people, they are cursed for being non-conformists, and so was the case with my best friend.

Still, despite the resistance that he faced, there was one thing that stood out in Vishesh – he never complained. Not even once. He was always calm, patient and undaunted, just like sitting at the back seat of my car, taking deep breaths lost in some world of his own desires, probably waiting to reach home after one hell of a tiring day.

It took us exactly one hour to reach Chandigarh from Punjabi University, Patiala. I dropped my friends, came home, freshened up quickly, had some milk and a sandwich, and set out again. I called the three of them one by one, informing them that I was coming to pick them up. The first stop was at Jaffy's, then Vishesh's, and finally we arrived in Sector 8 at Pujeet's place. They had already kept the bags outside the metal gate and someone or the other from his family was constantly running in out of the house, adding to the number. We helped loading what appeared to be an entire village's luggage, inside the car.

Then, like it happens in Hindi movies, Pujeet came out sobbing with his arms around his parents' shoulders, behaving almost like a bride about to leave with her husband. I felt like playing *'Baabul ki duaae…'* immediately on my phone. It aptly suited the situation.

In a few moments, the atmosphere got quite sombre. Pujeet lived in a joint family of twenty-three members and all of them got very emotional, sobbing as hard as they could, as if there was a contest to prove who was going to miss him the most. Neighbours peeped through the windows of their homes. All those aunties had their mouths covered with dupattas and were crying oceans.

"What are they so upset about?" I thought to myself, scanning Pujeet from head to toe, suspecting how this hairy man could be an object of such affection and attraction.

"Ask Pujji to tell these sexy aunties that his friends will take care of them," Jaffy whispered into my ear, rubbing his chest with soft intensity. "We will never let them miss him. Promise."

"If anyone hears your nonsense, I'll just pretend that I don't know you," I replied, trying to control my laughter.

Meanwhile, the baying of Pujeet and family carried on. Vishesh had to interfere and remind him that he was getting late for the bus. Wiping his tears, he bid adieu to his family after a few compulsory rituals.

Pujeet was now looking like a *sannyasi* leaving for the Himalayas. He had this vermilion *tilak* stretched till his hairline, and three yellow garlands around his neck, and I don't think he was in any mood to take them off too. Vishesh, Jaffy and I exchanged glances with each other, occasionally stealing a collective look at Pujeet, who looked insanely funny. Our very important discussion with him on the way was to make him promise to send us the latest iPhone by December end, behaving almost as if they were distributed for free in Canada.

Reaching ISBT-43, we dragged his luggage to the terminal, keeping all of it safely in the boot space of the Volvo bus. There were not many buses around and the four or five that were there didn't seem to be up for journey until the morning. Passengers began to get inside when the driver and helper got in, and the revving of the engine made some decent noise. A few ran out from the food court with cold drink bottles and rolls in their hands. They had to wrap up quicker than expected, it seemed.

We hugged Pujeet tight, controlling ourselves. Tears in one person's eyes would have rendered everyone to sob, and we being boys, sort of dislike looking weak (which is a wrong perception though). He waved at us standing at the door and we watched him settling down through the window. "Good bye, bro," we whispered.

The driver slowly steered the bus out, and there went our friend to live his destiny. Vishesh, Jaffy and I kept standing there, regardless of the bus having disappeared from our sight. It was a feeling of savagely hurting emptiness. And trust me, it pained real bad. So much so that for the next three hours, we were purposelessly driving on the Chandigarh-Manali road, without bothering to turn on the music, or uttering a single word.

It was precisely two in the morning when we decided to ride back to Jaffy's guest house in Mohali to get some sleep. Suddenly, we noticed a girl in the distance, signalling to us to stop. Her hair was loose and she looked dishevelled. She was wearing a sparkling micro mini skirt. That was surprising, as there was no disco or pub or party-house within a radius of at least fifty-sixty kilometres. We were not going to stop the car, fearing it was some sort of ploy to loot us. However, she fell flat, face down, and we jumped out, running to her. Vishesh reached near the girl and turned her face towards us. Her breath smelled of some serious levels of alcohol.

"Ma'am, are you alright?" he asked, softly slapping her face. She wasn't conscious. Vishesh repeated himself many more times. There was no answer. The girl opened her eyes and closed them again. We looked at each other wondering what to do. Leaving her alone like that would have been inhuman and our conscience didn't even allow that, but what action to take at an odd hour in a place far from the city for a girl who wasn't in her senses!

"We should inform the police," I rapidly suggested.

"First, let's get her behind the other side of the car," Jaffy said. The trucks that were passing by slowed down to see what was going on. They wouldn't know this girl had fallen on her own, and we'd end up looking like criminals.

"They didn't give my money," she mumbled as we helped her to sit against the back door.

"Who didn't give what?" Vishesh asked, drawing his ear closer to her lips.

"They screwed me together, and when I asked for payment, they threw me here," she said, mocking a childlike cry.

Jaffy and I traded an utterly shocked gape as if saying, "What? A prostitute!"

"Ma'am, we don't know about that, nevertheless we will drop you at your place. Where is it? Tell us," Vishesh said.

She smiled looking at him. "What about five thousand for two hours?"

"Ma'am, I don't want to get laid. Where is your home, tell us that."

"Alright! I'll give you a discount, sexy boy. Four thousand should be good," she said, winking

"Ma'am, I am asking where you live..."

"Okay, three k, sweet baby...and no bargaining now. I shall allow two of you to climb on me," she said to me and Vishesh.

"And me?" Jaffy mumbled.

The girl shook her head at him.

Jaffy almost suffered a heart attack. I tried controlling my laughter seeing the expression on his face. It was as if someone had taken out his intestines and sold them.

On the other hand, however, Vishesh wasn't amused. He stood up irritated, grousing something and tried to talk. As he sat down again to talk to the girl, she held him by the collar of his shirt.

"So should I consider the deal final?" she asked, coming closer to his lips all of a sudden.

"Have some shame, ma'am," Vishesh reacted, falling back. "I am bothered about your well-being and you are negotiating over your body. You are pathetic as hell."

She did not react for a moment and then her face had an expression as though she was about to break into tears.

Vishesh realised he had gotten too loud and as he was about to apologise, she abruptly began laughing.

"What the hell is going on?" I thought, scratching my head.

She spoke again, "Sir, let me tell you one thing. Once you go against your soul, it doesn't matter how many times you do it again. You never get killed twice. Also, no genuine girl in the world sells her body for leisure. It's not fun taking the load of several men. Especially when they treat you like a rag doll that can be twisted any way they want."

Her words moved us to shame. We were part of a selfishly insensitive world.

"I am so very sorry, ma'am," Vishesh said.

"If I had been born into a family like yours, I would have had friends like you with a thousand sweet memories to share. Now, I only find customers wanting to rip fun out of my flesh. So why not expect the same from you?"

A sense of guilt hit us all. We had our heads down in embarrassment.

"Take this, ma'am," Jaffy said. He had money in his hand. "This won't solve all your problems, but then giving this won't take anything away from me either."

We looked at him with pride. *You may act foolishly all the time, but this is the reason we love you, Jaffy. You are the nicest soul ever,* I said to myself.

The girl was a little hesitant, initially. But I guess, our honest intentions reflected on our faces, and convinced her. She accepted it, thanking us. "I shouldn't take this, but I will. My family won't get food for many days otherwise."

Vishesh and I did our bit too, and the girl had a brimming smile on her face, as if all her problems had come to an end. That day we learnt a very important lesson: There exist people in the world who are pushed into doing things due to constraints and compulsion. If all of us choose to help them overcome them and not manipulate their circumstances to our advantage, we'd help many lives to get out of the mess they continue to be in.

We dropped the girl at her house and got a few hours' sleep, after which we went to our respective homes. Jaffy and I continued with our resting spree, which, I guess, was going to go on for a lifetime as my father had a Zara showroom and Jaffy had three petrol pumps to his name. On the other hand, Vishesh, who had limited legacy to inherit, wasted no time and began to work on his novel. He was so bent on becoming a writer at the soonest that he had arrogantly ignored all our suggestions.

For almost a year, we had tried our best to convince him to earn money first, creating security for himself and his family and then go for his goal. He would rubbish our advice, replying with the same answer always. "Security created at the cost of happiness is an illusion that digresses us from our true purpose. It's like victory of an evil power over god's light within us."

His thoughts were always amazing and so was his mindset, perseverance and his rock solid focus. It was astounding, more so for us, to see a twenty-three-year-old with such maturity and passion, while most others of his age had sex, movies, alcohol, holidays and parties on their priority list. In spite of that, there was one person who always ridiculed him and his passion for writing, no matter what, claiming it to be a self-destructive activity that would bring an unbearable sense of guilt later. That person was his father.

Not that he wished anything bad for him, but Vishesh wasn't on the right path as per his experience. He was of the strong impression that his son was a reckless young boy who needed to be kept grounded and on a tight leash. And that evening, when Vishesh's struggle had truly begun, he got a taste of what exactly lay ahead for him.

"You are done with the farewell now. You wanted to go out last night, and I allowed you. Now please get a decent government job and set me free from my responsibilities," his father said.

"Please Papa, give me just one year. I earnestly want to give my dreams a shot."

"Listen Vishesh, you are getting carried away by the fame of authors like Chetan, Amish, Tushar, Ravi and others. But what you are intentionally ignoring, or you don't know because your knowledge is too poor, is the background these writers share in common. They come from the IITs. They have already proven that they are able and intellectual people, better than ninety-nine percent of India's population. They are licensed to succeed. And you on the other hand have been failing in maths and science right from the day you have been studying them. I always had to fold hands before your principal to get you through at the end of each year."

"Papa, I agree I was never academically good and I whole-heartedly apologise for that. I swear I tried my best in every class, but numbers and formulas always confused me. I used to write them twenty to thirty times while practicing, but during exams, I'd just forget them. Don't know why. But, you know, these students from tier-1 institutes, I have defeated the best of them in essay writing, debates, extempore, plays and every sort of literary competition, coming second to none."

"Judgment is never done fairly in these college level competitions, Vishesh. Grow up, for god's sake. They are manipulated by money and muscle power. Why do you keep irritating me with your moronic sense of logic?"

"But Papa, once people had tears in their eyes after my performance. It was so good that some of them even…"

"Shut up… Just shut the hell up! Go and prepare for bank exams or I'll break your laptop into pieces if you dare write a single word."

"Please, I request you. One chance is all I ask for."

"Every visit to your school for a parent-teacher meeting brought me humiliation for twelve straight years. You could never score well and instead of sincerely practising those subjects with complete concentration, you became a joker on stage to hide your weaknesses."

"No Papa, I only discovered what I was good at."

"I don't want to hit a grown-up boy. If you keep insisting any further, I won't hold back."

"I want you to be proud of me. And I know I'll never be able to do it through servitude, because I am not made for it. Just one year, Papa. Please." This was his only chance; he needed that time for himself and would do anything for it.

"Enough of your crap, Vishesh! I am not letting you sit at home for writing nonsense. I was quiet when you opted out of campus placements only because I thought you would learn a lesson seeing people of your age work hard and earn, and prepare for competitive papers. But you're quite thick-skinned. A stubborn boy who will only learn it the hard away. Anyhow, don't waste my time. Go to your room and I should be seeing you studying. And in case you are not interested in obeying me, you are more than welcome to leave my house." His father went back to his newspaper, marking an end to the discussion from his end.

Looking at the floor, heartbroken and attempting to control his nerves to explain, Vishesh walked back to his room. He switched off the lights and took deep breaths sitting in the corner, reminding himself that glory can never be achieved without struggle, and that lack of family support was going to be his hiccup to deal with. He had to find a way around it and wasn't complaining.

It took him a few minutes to get his focus straight and then he got up in high spirits, arranged the study table towards the east direction, took R.S. Aggarwal and a notebook out from the shelf, filled eight pages, quickly taping the examples, and then on the middle page of the notebook, began to complete his story. Soon he was so lost doing his work that he did not realise that his mother was standing right in front of him with a glass of milk. She kept it on the table. Vishesh didn't move.

She picked the glass up, and kept it back with a loud thud. Vishesh was still lost.

She went around to his back to verify what he was scribbling. Realising he wasn't doing what his father had instructed him to, she threw a few tight slaps on his head, yelling, "You are cheating us, boy, wasting precious time of your life; fooling us, acting over-smart, spoiling our old age, becoming an embarrassment to us. Why don't you die?"

Vishesh was so taken aback with this sudden uproar that he fell off from the chair, hurting his left arm and lower back. Meanwhile, his mother pulled the pages of the story out and tore them apart.

"Do this again and I'll call your father." She left, warning him.

It nevertheless brought no change to his mood and concentration. Though he did feel dejected for a while, he was habituated to such reactions. Until everyone slept, he pretended to be doing maths, this time keeping a Sidney Sheldon novel on his lap that he read, and when it was midnight, he took his phone in his mouth, put on the flashlight, collected the torn pieces of paper and slowly fixed them together and then typed the words on his laptop, dozing off happily as he finished his work.

The next day, he got up a little before sunrise, going for a run and carrying on pretending to be doing whatever kept his parents calm. They left for office at nine. Before finally leaving, one of them repeatedly made trips to Vishesh's room, making sure that their son was doing everything according to them.

He was also given homework to fill N number of pages with questions from maths chapters that he was studying (quite school boy kind of stuff that was!) before they were back, and that it would be checked. Vishesh bribed his younger sister with a hundred rupees and two *samosas*, and got his work done before the deadline. His sister could exactly copy his handwriting.

I called Vishesh in the evening.

"Are we meeting?" I asked as he picked my call within two rings.

"No excuse to come out," he replied.

"Till when is this drama going to last?" I asked, pissed off.

"Till I am able to earn and make dad happy," he replied.

"This means we are never meeting, right?" I said.

"At least not today, mate," he said.

"Think of something, please. I am dying of boredom," I requested.

"Why don't you come over to my place?" he suggested.

"I am shit scared of your dad, man. He stares at me like ACP Pradyuman from that TV serial *CID*," I said.

"Don't worry. I'll get you inside from the back door," he said. "Just remember to call me when you reach."

"Umm…Okay. Give me fifteen minutes," I said.

"Bring Kaamdev (which was a nickname for Jaffy) along, I need to ask him something," he said.

"He won't be coming. He has gone to the police station," I informed him.

"Police station?" He was surprised.

"His brother was caught eve-teasing in the afternoon. The cops have thrown him into jail," I said.

"My god! The entire family is full of perverts," he remarked before hanging up.

"Come on in," Vishesh said, carefully opening the gate to avoid any sound.

"Should I take my slippers off?" I checked with him, noticing the wet floor.

"Keep them on. It's perfectly fine," he said.

"Man, how can your room be so clean?" I asked as I stepped inside. It gave vibes of some saint's hut.

"I can't write sitting around in a mess. It distracts me," he replied as we both sat down on the bed.

"How much work left on the book?" I asked

"Halfway through! Will most likely be able to complete the final draft by the end of September," he shared happily.

"Wow! What next? Any publisher shortlisted?" I wanted to know more now.

"I am not Twinkle Khanna or Karan Johar with that kind of privilege. In fact, I am nobody. I'll have to send the script to big and small publishing houses and later decide depending on their response."

"Alright!" I said, "And hey, what about Nishtha's birthday? Any plans?"

"You guys chatted?" he asked

"Not in that regard. Why, any problem?"

"Please avoid anything of that sort with her. I don't think I'll be able to arrange a party this time or even go to one if it is arranged by someone else," he said a little sadly.

"Mark my words, you are going to die," I said. When do girlfriends understand all this, I wondered.

"I'll try to make her understand," he said.

"Yeah right! You think you can do that?" I asked, making fun.

"You buddy, you'll calm her down. It's your duty," he said.

"No no no no no! I am not getting into this. Why should I do the dirty work? Am I running a free of cost counselling agency for troubled couples that each time they have issues, they come to me, seeking help? You will have to find a way to go, plus it'll be wrong on your part to escape it, that's it. End of the story."

"I have no other option. If I take a step outside the house and mom and dad come to know about it, they will nail me first and then fight between themselves blaming each other's parents and my birth for everything that has gone wrong in the last twenty-five years of their marriage." He had said it very matter-of-factly, but it was hard to imagine how someone could live in an environment like that.

"How do you live with such parents, I wonder?"

"They aren't bad, Dhruv. They have been through a lot in life. My dad, even today, buys me branded shoes without asking, and for the last five years, has been wearing the same Ludhiana-made hard sport shoes."

"You are inspired by Heera, right? He is your role model, isn't he?" I asked him.

"Who Heera?" Vishesh looked on, confused.

"The son in the movie *Sooryavansham*," I told him.

"The one which Set Max is completely crazy for?" He smiled after a long time.

"Exactly...," I said, laughing.

Our conversation went on and we went for a short walk outside, having coke and cheese burgers in a small confectionery nearby. I shared how depressing it felt at the very thought of sitting at the cash counter of my showroom for fifteen to sixteen hours every day for the rest of my life, calculating the success ratio of salesmen on even national holidays. My party days were over and I had to take the responsibility off my dad's shoulders, making his comfort my priority.

Vishesh motivated me, suggesting an all-time best alternative that in case I didn't feel like doing it or the sales went to zero given his faith in my ability, I could sell the shop for millions, get a fixed deposit for the sum and live on the interest forever. I laughed out loud, asking him to keep his Plan B to himself, or it would send my father straight to heaven.

Towards the end, when I was about to leave, I tried convincing him that he shouldn't miss Nishtha's birthday at any cost. And in case he was prudently sure of not going, he must mentally prepare her or she would be hurt later. He, pondering over it for a moment, promised to responsibly handle it.

So keeping my words in mind, Vishesh pinged her later that night:

Someone is too busy, no?

Nishtha: *Look who's talking. The one who hurriedly cuts the phone saying 'will call back in two minutes' and appears days later, acting over-smart.*

Vishesh: *I am so sorry, love. You know my parents, no? They are always over-worried, and sort of gang up on me if they find me doing anything they feel is unproductive.*

Nishtha: *I didn't know you categorise our relationship into 'An Unproductive Activity.' Wonderful!*

Vishesh: *Baby, I am not saying that.*

Nishtha: *Are you sure you love me? I feel like an option to you. You talk when you are free, and I suffer, as you seldom care, even when I need you so much.*

Vishesh: *Nishtha, please understand. It's difficult to talk with Mom and Dad around.*

Nishtha: *I am a girl, Vishesh. I have to answer to my parents more than you ever will have to. But because I consider you my priority, I devote my time without having you ask for it.*

Vishesh: *I know it's completely my fault, Nishtha, and justifying myself right now is no less than giving a petty excuse. Trust me, I have no world beyond you and writing. It's just that when Mom and Dad go to office, I try making most of that time as when they return, they keep a hawk's eye on me, making writing almost impossible.*

Nishtha: *Alright then. Focus on your work. Goodnight. I love you!*

Vishesh: *Please listen, I didn't mean to hurt you.*

Nishtha: *Right now I am watching the climax of* The Fault in Our Stars *and feeling wonderful about love. Kindly don't spoil my mood... let's talk later.*

Vishesh: *Sure. I won't want to be The Peter Van Houten of your life. You expect so much, but all you get in the end is crap.*

Nishtha: *Done with your emotional drama?*

Vishesh: *Only if it has worked in my favour.*

Nishtha: *Remember I had wanted us to watch this movie together? I missed it out because of you and now I have to see it alone on my stupid laptop.*

Vishesh: *Consider it as a long term investment, baby. I'll be taking you to special screenings of all the films you wish to see. I'll be that huge for you. I promise.*

Nishtha: *There was a man who used to say to his wife, let me be number one in the nation and I'll give you all my time. After achieving that, he said let me become number one in the world and you shall have me. Poor girl died waiting somewhere in the middle of his frenzy. I guess I will end up like that.*

Vishesh: *Nishtha, nothing of this sort will happen. Although I had this dream of becoming a writer since my childhood, your presence has made a huge difference. Baby, I wish to win for 'us' now. It suddenly no longer matters what people who underrated me or declared me a born failure think. More important than proving them wrong, is seeing you happy. And the tool for me to make it happen is to succeed at writing. I need to put in a lot of hard work for that. I know I am expecting a lot involving you in a dream that may never come true. Nevertheless, I want to try, and without your support, I won't be able to get through. I promise I will make up for everything that you lose because of me today.*

Nishtha: *I have all my faith in you, Vishesh. I apologise for being selfish and not understanding. I am sure you will do your best and achieve all that you wish to.*

Vishesh: *Yes, Nishtha. With you by my side, I am bound to succeed, and undoubtedly, I will make up for every single thing. Even your birthday that I will miss.*

Nishtha: *Excuse me?*

Vishesh: *Baby, Actually no....*

Nishtha: *Actually what?*

Vishesh: *First promise you won't get angry.*

Nishtha: *Actually what, Vishesh fucking Raghav?*

Vishesh: *I won't be able to come for your birthday.*

Nishtha: *What a beautiful way to fool me! Go to hell! No need to wish me either. Bye.*

Texting that, Nishtha must have switched off her phone as none of Vishesh's messages got delivered. He waited for an hour for her response, checking his phone every thirty seconds, but in vain. He put his phone on the side and lay on the bed, unable to get any sleep. It wasn't like he was agitated on himself or too bothered as he was sure Nishtha would empathise, sooner or later. It was simply one of those nights where you don't have any reason to not be able to sleep, and yet you are not able to.

✦

THE ONE FROM THE STARS

THE NEXT DAY, VISHESH WAS AT THE DINING TABLE HAVING breakfast with his family. His sister who could barely gulp a bite without the television on, tuned into Zee Cinema where the year 2007's most successful and touching movie *Taare Zameen Par* was being showcased. The movie had reached the point where Nikumbh (Amir Khan) explains to Ishaan's father what his son's problem (Dyslexia) exactly was, and how the kid was suffering living under an undiagnosed, and most importantly, a misunderstood state.

"Should we take him to a doctor too, Ritu?" Vishesh's father said. "I mean, after explaining so much, if he is unable to distinguish between good and bad, he must be mentally ill like this boy."

"I am rather in favour of going to some astrologer to get his *kundli* seen," his mother replied. "This sinister boy born on an eclipse, I am afraid, will get our reputation to the ground."

"I had never thought life would come to a point where I'll have to escape answering my friends' question on this disgrace's career," his father went on almost venomously.

"With me, it's even worse, Hari. I have stopped talking to everyone at office. I avoid any sort of eye contact with the neighbours and keep away from all parties I am invited to. It will be such a shame to tell them we have a donkey sitting at home doing nothing," his mother added more insult to the injury.

"Bad karma in our past life," summed up his father.

"See Neelam Agnihotri's son now, Google has taken him for a package of ninety-five lakhs. I can only imagine his family's reaction when he'll receive the first salary alert on his phone: Your account has been credited with almost nine lakhs. Nine lakhs, Hari…nine lakhs! Mrs Agnihotri will dance upside down in the colony. She will be purchasing gold every month, whereas my blood pressure will keep falling seeing the rising gold price."

"It's all destiny, Ritu. Maybe we will end up selling off everything to settle down this idiot."

"Then also, do you think he will spare us? He will consume us from head to toe."

Vishesh's parents didn't stop ridiculing him. They went on and on. Meanwhile, he, chewing slowly, feeling guilty, glare fixed at the plate, controlling his tears, chose not to answer back. But there was one thing he was unable to understand throughout: What wrong was he doing? He wasn't charged for a murder that had caught national attention; didn't rape anyone, nor tried flying to Syria to join ISIS? Then why this intense disapproval towards the path he had chosen? Why the huge concern regarding what society thought and not how alone their own flesh and blood would feel in pursuit of his dreams?

Being parents, Mr and Mrs Raghav had every damn right to criticise their son, motivate him in any manner they felt was appropriate, but sometimes, the child is in need of appreciation, encouragement, faith and certainly not humiliating comparisons.

I mean, take a moment and imagine a situation where a person has been diagnosed with cancer. The patient and his entire family are bound to be tormented, dragooned and feel broken like hell. But the fear in the patient's mind is going to be far more than that of anyone else, no matter how much he/she is loved or cared for.

A patient very strong at heart may not show it, but clearly, the chemo, the hope, the desperation to live that they go through, is deeply impacting them from inside. In the same way, for the one walking an unconventional path, giving up on the pleasures of a normal life is not easy. They sacrifice thousands of small things that no one cares to take notice of. Yet, they don't complain and show a bigger heart. No kind of fear is able to intimidate them. They don't stop dreaming, irrespective of the iron-packed and insurmountable challenges waiting ahead. In fact, they bravely opt to fight like a true hero.

Should such people be inspired or should they be continuously tarnished? The former fuels the passion and makes them feel wanted, while the latter may lead to laying the foundation of their destruction.

Remember, not everyone is meant to be number one. Not everyone finds a place in record books. That nevertheless, in no sense, makes the person who tries and falls, any less of a champion, especially because, one: Majority of the world has got no clue about their inner calling. Two: Very few out of those who know what they are made for, show the courage to pursue their dreams.

Vishesh, like every other day, came back to his room feeling dejected, spent a few minutes relaxing, checked through the window if his parents had left, recollected himself and began to do his work.

One-and-a-half years later…

Times had changed dramatically and so had our idea of life and opinions. The boy who once looked all ready for a grander stage and fame, was collapsing and tumbling. The line of his career graph that was expected to rise like a phoenix was falling like a house of cards. But irrespective of the obstacles, Vishesh had finally completed writing his book. It was, surprisingly for us, turned down by almost all the publishers in the country and every second response to his submission in his mail box read:

THE ONE FROM THE STARS

Dear Mr Vishesh,

Thank you for your interest in publishing with us. We have evaluated your submission and regret to inform you that it does not, at present, fit our publishing list. We wish you luck in finding a suitable publisher.

While a few houses did offer to publish him, it was always on a condition for him to buy back one thousand copies, which nearly required one lakh rupees. A couple of them also offered the condition of bearing the distribution cost, requiring to pay the same amount, which his father had straightaway declined.

What was more unfortunate was that one of the literary agents had gone on to say something as extreme as:

Your work, Mr Vishesh, is far from publishable. Thus, we won't be able to represent you. Kindly let us know if you are looking for editorial services or a detailed critique.

It must have been harrowing for him to have been turned down so obnoxiously. God knows how those insensitive remarks would have shaken him from within. Most of all because Vishesh had given up every single thing for writing, and now he was being told that he wasn't fit to write. That would have made him think of quitting immediately. But strikingly, Vishesh ignored it all, saying that it was okay, as after all, who on earth was he to judge. An opinion of a single person was hardly to be taken very seriously.

In addition to that, Hari Lal Uncle, on behalf of his son, had forcefully filled all government job screening exams that came out during all those months and Vishesh had flunked in all of them. Let alone getting close to the overall cut-offs, there wasn't any paper, I remember, in which he had scored more than the minimum required. On the other hand, his love life was suffering too, for he hadn't spared much time for Nishtha, asking her to wait, wait and wait. If she requested for an outing, he was unable to go, or even if he managed to go, he had limited time, which annoyed her to an extent that she had stopped calling him to meet up.

All of us, his friends, concluded that he had done a huge blunder and that his crazy persistence would be the end of him. We had lost patience with Vishesh. The childlike enthusiasm we used to show for the fulfilment of his wishes had now turned into what we called maturity. Participating and winning in college competitions was so different from trying to turn it into a profession, we realised. It was almost impossible to make it happen. Behind his back, all of us were criticising him for being so adamant. For us, following a dream was okay, but not keeping a plan B ready was sort of starting to sound stupid. Almost each one of us from the batch were doing reasonably well, except for him.

But despite all the gloominess around, Vishesh believed, saying to us, "It's never about these several 'no's that count, it is one 'yes' that will, and I promise to take this to the point where every house that has rejected me, will repent missing out on an author who will matter soon."

We argued with him, forcing him to think of an alternative in case things didn't work out. He was least bothered about the consequences, explaining to us with examples of people like Sergeant Colonel, Jack Ma, Abraham Lincoln, and Nelson Mandela, dead set on proving to us that adversity is important before tasting victory and that giving up and escaping should never be an option. Moreover, he wasn't in favour of having any substitute plans. For him, his work was his oxygen. It was his breath and he wasn't thinking of anything else, no matter how many failures hit him and tried to destroy him. He was holding on tightly to his dreams and was patiently waiting for his time to come.

Not sure if it was his resilience or ego, I prayed for a positive response from the last publisher who was yet to reply. Basically, it was a small, yet a decent publishing house, whose books, if not available at a lot of places, at least saw presence in half of the stores in India. But before we could know if they were accepting his work or not, there was something else that waited for Vishesh.

He had been referred to a psychiatrist, to which his father did not want to go as he didn't believe in all that stuff. But on insistence of his closest doctor friend, who was a regular visitor to their home and had noticed certain behaviour patterns of Vishesh like repeatedly making a huge fuss about washing hands for no apparent reason, he agreed. Only to discover that his son was suffering from Obsessive Compulsive Disorder.

"Tell me very clearly," Vishesh's father said to the psychiatrist. "Do you want to bring in a blue van that we see in

Hindi films, put him in that and take him to Agra or Amritsar, into an asylum?"

"Sir, OCD is not that. It is, please understand, a problem in which a person has uncontrollable, reoccurring thoughts in which they feel the urge to repeat a thing over and over. In simpler words, if you need to decipher, it is when a person is unable to control their thoughts."

"Basically this means he is mad? I mean, if you do something for no reason, again and again, it's madness, isn't it?"

"Mad is the most disastrous word that you can use, sir. Don't do this," the psychiatrist tried to caution.

"By the way, what do your books say? Why does it happen? Like eating more of junk food or something like that is the cause?" Hari Lal Uncle asked.

"No sir, it is caused by an imbalance of the brain chemical called serotonin, or it could be genetic as well."

"Since he was ten, I have been giving him twelve almonds every day, and that I believe negates the first reason. As for the second one, in our entire family, not a single person has ever had such an illness."

"Mr Hari Lal, I understand your concern, but I can't deny what I have diagnosed."

"Okay, if for a minute I agree to what you are saying, what do we need to do, kindly explain?"

"Most importantly, give your son independence, a shoulder to cry on when needed, listen to him when he wants you to. Along with that, we will begin his behaviour and medication therapy, and with god's grace, he will get better soon," the psychiatrist explained.

"I should listen to him? Give him independence? Are you crazy or what? Tomorrow you will say let him become a writer also. Give him one lakh rupees to get his book published. And then he will be fine, right? This is what you want to say?"

"Sir, you are mixing your ego with facts and that…"

"Doctor Sahib, enough! The only thing I am sure of is we don't need your services. And from your comments I have understood that since he is sitting idle at home for the last one-and-a-half years, he is behaving oddly. From tomorrow, he will go to work and will be absolutely fine. I don't believe in diseases that Englishmen created to loot money, simple! Baba Ramdev says yoga helps to control the entire body's functioning. I'll make him do that if required, and he'll be okay." Hari Lal Uncle got up haughtily without wasting any more time, and Vishesh followed him to the car.

Fastening his seat belt, his father slapped the steering furiously. "I am getting a job arranged for you. If you don't do it, just get the hell out of my life. You have frustrated me to the core." He added, louder this time, "Troubling me always… am I meant for that only? I should bear all the frustration in office, and then it's you who at this age has brought me to my knees."

Just as Hari Lal Uncle had settled on the couch rubbing his face, tired, his wife shouted from the kitchen asking, "What happened? What did the doctor say?"

"He said that your boy is suffering from OCD."

"What is that?"

"Some sort of mental illness."

"If for the whole day he will sit in front of his mobile and laptop, then these CD/DVD kind of diseases are bound to happen," his mother said.

"Nothing has happened to him, he is just a free mind with no work to do and that's it. Get ready quickly. We have to leave for your brother's house. I have talked to him, he is at home."

"Why are we going there?"

"I have to get a job arranged for this idiot," he said pointing at Vishesh who stood at the door of the hall.

"What can he do about it?"

"Ritu, he is now the head HR in Janobs Life Insurance."

"Oh yeah! How could I forget about his recent promotion? Give me five minutes, I'll get ready."

Vishesh's parents instructed him to not take advantage of their absence and leave with his friends since his sister would be alone in the house and that they should have dinner early and sleep on time and not waste it watching movies. Having locked the gate as they left, he came to his room, bolted the door and took out all his diaries from the shelf.

He opened them one by one, glancing through the poems, short stories and everything that he had written. He put his fingertips on the words and pondered over what wrong he had done to be failing so much. Where was the mistake in all the dedication that he had shown? Vishesh paused in between, closing his eyes, imagining reading out his work to a crowd of people who were his loyal readers. He was a very successful author in that world. It brought a slight smile to his face. At the end of the session, he signed books for all the people and upon returning home, his parents affectionately hugged him with their chests swollen, very proud of the achievements of their child.

It hurt Vishesh to return to reality. Seeing his father's concern that day, not only did he feel ashamed of himself, he seemed to be running short of hope as well. He thought about how his friends had bought gifts for their parents with their first salary, publishing it gloriously on Facebook, and how they spent their holidays and festivals at exotic locations, while he sat at home, waiting for his time. And yet, he could do nothing except be a burden, giving not even a single reason to make his parents happy.

It was quite unlike him to have felt that, but low moments are a part of life. Just when he was about to gather himself, reminding that his struggle was nothing in comparison to what so many legends had suffered and that he should keep his fight going, he received Nishtha's text on his phone.

I urgently need to meet you tomorrow. Kindly spare five minutes, it's a very humble request.

Vishesh: *Mom-Dad not at home tonight. We can meet now, if you say.*

Nishtha: *That would be great.*

Vishesh: *I will give you a missed call as soon as I reach your door. Come out, okay?*

Nishtha: *No, don't come to my house. Let me meet you on the road opposite Piccadilly Square.*

Vishesh: *I don't think it's safe for you. It's secluded, especially during the evenings. Let's meet somewhere else.*

Nishtha: *No time to argue about safety and all. I need to see you at the earliest. Reach on time please.*

Vishesh: *Okay, I am coming.*

Nishtha was already waiting for him when he reached. She had parked her car on the side, and there wasn't any vehicle to be seen on the road. The sun was almost down and it would be dark soon. She jumped out as soon as she saw Vishesh's bike approaching. Vishesh stopped his bike right in front of Nishtha's car.

Taking off his helmet and putting it on the seat carefully, he hugged her and said, "What is it, love? Everything okay?"

She nodded her head, half smiling. It seemed a forced smile though.

"Vishesh, I want to tell you something really important. Don't get mad, be patient, don't react hastily, and try and understand." It felt she was almost preparing ground for something serious, and Vishesh felt himself go stiff with worry.

"What happened, dear? Why are you speaking so fast? Calm down."

She hesitated for a while.

"Listen..." she began, and then took her time, making Vishesh anxious. He was worried as she seemed pretty grave.

"What is it that she wants to say in the middle of nowhere?" he thought

"We can't be together anymore..." she managed to let it out.

"What?" was all his shocked mind could gather.

"It's the end of our relationship," she confirmed.

"What are you saying?"

"Vishesh, I am sorry, it's over."

"Did I do anything wrong? Hey, tell me, I'll fix it, I promise," he softly asked, holding her face in his hands.

She put his hands away, replying, "My parents have been looking for a guy for me and despite my repeated requests to you to find a way to be together, you have been asking for more time."

"Yes dear, and that's only because I want to be..."

She cut him short, "Yes, you want to be a writer, settle down, earn a little before taking my responsibility! I have heard all this crap before, Vishesh. But I simply can't tell that to my parents. You are twenty-five and earning no money. I don't think I am secure with you."

"Nishtha, please. I love you."

"You do, but something else is your priority more than I am."

"No, Nishtha. That's not true," he tried his best.

"I wish it wasn't, Vishesh... I really wish. And had you been madly in love with me, like I am, I too would have been given equal importance and never ignored. Also, don't mind my words, but you have been thoroughly selfish all these years. You didn't think of your parents, of me, of us; crazily running after a stupid dream that made no sense because all you care about is fame and nothing else."

He was left speechless at her words, which pierced through his heart.

She continued, "All my friends go out to party with their men. They relax, they love, they travel, share problems, spend quality time together. And we…what do we do? Nothing! Why? Because sometimes your father is there, sometimes your mother is there, and other times you are working. Every time, you have an excuse for not meeting me. Every single fucking time you have a justification. Where am I in all of this? Tell me! Where? Chase whatever you want now, I don't mind, but I can't sacrifice beyond this. I want a normal man with normal needs… And I didn't want to tell you this to hurt you, but a boy had come to see me today and we exchanged rings. The marriage has been fixed for next week. Everything has happened all of a sudden and even I wasn't expecting it."

Having said that, she looked around for a while, maybe gathering courage, and then showed the ring on her finger.

Tears welled up in his eyes. He almost choked, gently stepping back in disbelief.

"Take care, Vishesh. Good luck for your future. I hope you at least get what you have ignored us all for." Those were her last words, and then she walked off, unable to look him in the eyes, and drove away.

He stood there frozen, obliterated. His glare locked in on the car that speedily vanished out of his sight. Perhaps it was the last time he saw the girl with whom he had painted dreams of his future.

I don't know why after so much of trust and co-operation, Nishtha ended up thinking so negatively about Vishesh. The truth was that whenever Vishesh talked of the days that would follow after the accomplishment of his goals, he always imagined her along. Always. Moreover, success never had the same meaning for Vishesh after he began to see Nishtha. Vishesh wasn't fighting to become wealthy or famous. He simply used to say that if he was able to fulfil Nishtha's every wish through his work, he would consider the purpose of his life fulfilled.

I wished she could have been a little more patient with him. Nevertheless, with all due respect, she had her reasons too. Vishesh blamed himself for what had happened and quietly walked into an empty space thinking that he deserved no love. Surprisingly, on the outside, he didn't show he was in any sort of pain, saying to all of us that she had taken a smart decision, as her 'to-be-husband' would certainly be incredibly rich, and able to offer her much better.

Jaffy and I humbly requested him to at least not think himself unworthy. He ignored us, explaining that in his pursuit of excellence, he would have deprived her of small moments of joy. She had made the right choice as she didn't deserve to be subjected to someone's struggle, and that in this one life, all she must get is love.

Though we still expected an outburst of some kind on the day of her wedding, nothing happened, except for writing for an unusually longer time to deviate his mind and not with the intention of getting published or something.

Also, the last publication house that we had expectations from had sent a similar email of regret. Every option had now faded into oblivion. Vishesh did not show any visible reaction this time too. Evidently, after all the denials, rejections and failures, he had mastered the art of hiding his emotions. He had understood that there were many ears to listen to his words, but no heart to understand his feelings. In the end, everybody only wanted you to speak, for they in exchange wanted you to listen to them and agree to their point of view.

A WEEK LATER, AS ARRANGED ON THE RECOMMENDATION OF his maternal uncle, Vishesh appeared for an interview with Janobs Life Insurance. He cracked it easily and was all set to join them the next day in the role of a Relationship Manager. His relatives poured in to congratulate, and his parents were satisfied as if their son had won India a gold medal in the Olympics. Sweets were being distributed, coconuts and oil was being offered in the temple, and god was being thanked as if he was one of the panel members who had selected Vishesh for the job.

In between all of this, I wondered why couldn't anyone notice Vishesh's sadness and ask the reason. Why couldn't anyone figure out that apparent sense of unhappiness and brokenness, or were they intentionally ignoring it? Maybe yes, they were.

After all, for them, more significant was the victory of their idea of false security and materialism, and there was no better occasion to be ecstatic about successfully slaughtering an inner voice and dragging a vision down to their everyday state of insecurities and fears. The good for nothing society, only good at admiring people on television, had crushed one more among them who had passionately stood up showing symptoms of conquering the impossible.

Vishesh's fate was sealed as he stood staring at his reflection in the mirror – hair neatly combed, face properly shaven, and the body covered in a pair of blue trousers and a white shirt with a matching tie. Ready to go to the place where he had never planned to set foot – office. As he came out of his room, his mother called him to bow down before the photo of his grandparents. He ignored her and kept walking. His father shouted from behind, telling him to come back and touch his feet. He did not bother about that too. Lost in disappointment, he went on.

Stopping his bike in the Sector 47D parking, Vishesh turned around looking at all the boards, figuring out his workplace, and placing it among the high rise buildings, he stared at it releasing a breath, trying to come to terms with reality. Entering inside nervously, Vishesh found the first and second table empty. The computers were on, but there wasn't anyone there. He went to the third one. The same thing. His eyes then fell on the glass cubicle in the corner. It was sound proof. There were four people standing with their heads down and one person who seemed to be their boss, sat on the chair indicating towards the board behind, shouting her throat out. She was a lady, probably in her late-thirties or early forties.

He stood waiting for them to finish. The manager's attention, in between, switched to him and following her instruction, one of the RMs hurried out asking, "Yes sir, how can we help you?"

"I was supposed to be joining today," he replied.

The manager called him inside. She had already received an email that a new employee would be joining.

"You are Mr Vishesh Raghav?" she confirmed as he got inside the cubicle.

"Yes, ma'am," he replied slowly.

"I am privileged to welcome you to the most prestigious sales team of Chandigarh," she said, shaking hands with him. "I am the branch manager here, Pooja Garg."

"Honoured to meet you, ma'am."

Then a little introduction with the team happened and they were back to talking business. Since Vishesh hadn't received a formal training about working and the products, Ms Garg assigned a buddy to him in Rahul Singla – a short guy with buried eyes and no neck, but very sharp in appearance. He had been with the company from more than a year and was a street-smart player at achieving targets. For the first half of the working hours that day, he kept Vishesh along, taking him on calls, practically explaining responsibilities and how the work was done.

Vishesh was flummoxed seeing the way he pitched life insurance. He right away knew he could not do it that way. More so, because Rahul Singla wasn't ethically securing the customer's future, he was neatly shaving them from tip to toe. In his commercial spirit, he ignored the actual needs of the people, focusing on products that would fetch him a promotion and gift hampers.

To Vishesh, he suggested while riding his Activa back to office in the afternoon after attending to a customer, "Find five-six *murgas* (potential customers), and chop their heads off. Bangkok Tour Contest is waiting. This is the opportunity to get a sponsored sandwich massage or whatever horny stuff you would like."

"Now I know why people in India are allergic to the term 'Life Insurance'. Seventy percent of the population already doesn't have a cover, and the ones who do, are getting their hands burnt every day, thanks to the priorities of a few agents like you," Vishesh told him.

Rahul laughed. "If you have a better way of selling, why don't you teach me as well?"

"I am least interested in all this nonsense," Vishesh said.

"Okay? So what are you interested in?" Rahul asked. "Washing your hands at the customers' place after every fifteen to twenty minutes, behaving as if you are a mechanic? Is that it?"

"That's just a hygiene check, dude. Don't make fun. And speak slowly, I can feel drops of your saliva on my face," Vishesh retorted.

"Get used to it, mate. I am doing it unintentionally. Boss will knowingly do it every day to get the work done."

"You are kidding me, right?" Vishesh confirmed.

"No! I am telling you to always keep this helmet on. Even while sitting in the office."

Vishesh was irked.

"Where am I stuck? What am I to do? My entire life that was once floating with stories and fantasy is now down to chasing targets to keep this job , only to make my parents feel honoured among the people they don't even like. Why can't I just run off, far away from everyone?" Vishesh muttered to himself.

"Did you say something?" asked Rahul.

"No," Vishesh replied.

He muttered again. Being a little dramatic this time. "Parents are god, they say. Who are we then? Slaves to what they feel is right? We are fools? Jerks? Having no sense of right or wrong? Can't we fail and try again?"

People who passed by on their vehicles, stared at him thinking he was mad. Some even cackled. Rahul pressed the brakes, looking back in Vishesh's eyes and asking, "Buddy, what are you doing?"

"What am I doing?"

"Whom are you talking to, fellow? People go crazy after working for at least a few months in the market. You are already a defective piece."

"Sorry sorry! I was chanting the *Hanuman Chalisa*," Vishesh lied.

"Do it at home, Pandit ji," Rahul said, sternly this time. "Don't reduce me to a laughing stock along with you."

Reaching office, he was in person trained by the manager until closing time, and was also allotted a database of seven hundred people whom he needed to call every now and then and pitch financial products. He had to double his focus to be able to understand her as everything was passing over his head. He was getting a severe headache thinking what he was going to do for the rest of his life. Selling products and chasing people to buy them at the soonest wasn't him. It was nowhere close to being the boy nature had made him like. The very idea of working in such an alien field was shaking his confidence.

To sum up Vishesh's first day's learning: He should throw benevolence out of himself and deceive anyone and everyone, because if he won't, some other agent from a different company would.

We felt apprehensive when Vishesh told us about the day in the evening. Not that we were absolute saints who would never cheat on anyone if required, but he was a person tailor-made for observing different characters, placing himself in their shoes and putting down whatever he could weave out of it on paper. How could a person with such traits be expected to trick, mislead and lie for his targets? His working in such an industry was like using a cricket bat to play tennis. Could anyone win a game doing that? There simply stood no chance.

Even Jaffy had this much of common sense to agree.

"Isn't it, Kaamdev?" I said as the three of us sat on the black air mattress, leaning against the wall of my room. Vishesh had come directly to my place from his office.

"Absolutely, and I am telling you, Vishesh," Jaffy answered, "Leave this job, or I fear you might commit suicide."

"Do you both know a good method of dying?" Vishesh asked, "so that I can reach heaven without much pain."

Jaffy said, "Hang yourself!"

"I am asking for a painless method, dude," Vishesh said.

"It's just a matter of two minutes, bro. A real man can handle that, trust me," Jaffy said

"Would you mind giving me a demo please?" Vishesh said.

"Stop this rubbish, guys," I interrupted. "And whom are you listening to, Vishesh? This man? Who wakes up to the sound of his own fart? Bloody self-appointed consultant giving people stupid advices!"

"No matter who it is, everyone is always scolding me," Jaffy fought back. "My father, mother, brother, sister, friends, everyone. I don't want to stay here. Bye."

He tramped through the door in anger. We shouted for him to return, but he wouldn't listen.

Two minutes later, he came back running.

"What happened now? I thought you didn't want to stay," I asked.

"There are stray dogs roaming outside."

"Really? Why didn't you join them? They will be happy to have their brother back," I said.

"Shut up!" he shouted, and then getting on his knees, holding my hand, softly requested, "Drop me to the end of the main road, please."

"Sit here first. Pujeet is about to video call," I said. "Let's talk, we will see about you later."

"I'll wash my hands and come," Vishesh said, getting up.

"Was it inside your underwear that you have to do it every ten minutes?" I asked, ruffled.

Vishesh hurried back rubbing his hand on his pants as Pujeet came on FaceTime. All of us cheered as he got live on the screen. He was twirling his moustache, smiling seeing us together. His hair was a bit messed up as if he had just woken up from bed and he had gained some extra kilos on the cheeks. In the background, there was a neatly painted yellow wall.

"Friend! How have you been?" I began.

"Living out my fated time," Pujeet replied

"We thought you were partying in Canada and getting laid?" Jaffy said.

"These days I am cleaning toilets to keep my body and soul together," Pujeet said.

"Really?" Jaffy said, disgusted.

"Come on, man. What's bad about it?" I said, grabbing Jaffy by the belly fat. "No work is big or small. It's the thinking that is."

"Yes, no work is big or small, I agree," Jaffy said.

"Don't fake this maturity to encourage me, alright? I know our typical mindset and what you are going to discuss right after this call. You will all be saying 'Poor Pujeet! Life has come down to cleaning toilets for him.' And then you all will be feeling positive about not coming here, concluding, 'We took a smart decision of staying in our country. At least we don't have to take care of someone else's shit'."

"No, brother. We don't talk like that about you," Vishesh said.

"Have humans ever let an opportunity slip to feel good about their life by pointing out the negativity in someone else's?" Pujeet countered.

"Well, that's a great point. I am impressed, Mr Philosopher," said Jaffy.

"But guys, let me do away with the loan that dad took for me, and I'll come back. It just doesn't feel good here," Pujeet said

"What happened, mate? All well?" Vishesh asked concerned.

"I made a mistake, I guess. It feels very lonely over here. No one has time to stop and listen. Was wondering…when I turn fifty and need you all for me, no one will be able to come. I'll die wishing to see you all for one last time," Pujeet said

"Pujji, are you crying mate?" I asked

That question triggered him more. He put his head down, hiding his face.

"Pujji, what happened, bro?" Jaffy asked

He nodded his head, wiping tears.

"Hey, hero, what's the issue? Won't you share it with your brothers, huh?" I asked.

He looked up after a while and said in a trembling tone, "Granny passed away a day before."

"What?" The three of us said in unison.

"It felt so miserably helpless sitting here. I mean, I couldn't do anything except consoling everyone over the phone, thinking how they would be dealing with the loss. Wish I could pack and come back right away. Granny used to say every day, Pujji, it's my last wish to see you getting married, my child, but I... such a selfish grandson of hers. Couldn't even lend my shoulder to carry her body."

A brief silence followed.

"In pursuit of earning what's not mine, I lost what was given to me. Never will I commit such a mistake again. Never," Pujeet said, sobbing like an innocent child.

"Don't let yourself be weak, Pujji," Jaffy said. "This might not be the right time to keep emotions over logic. Maybe you feel guilty for not being present with your family. Do they think the same? Do they blame you the way you are blaming yourself? I don't think so. And since the lifestyle you wanted can only be lived where you are, no one should be upset about your absence. You proposed it to your family, they happily agreed. That's simple. You cannot be everywhere and do everything. You will have to let go of a few things on the way. More importantly, when you were about to fly, didn't you know if anything like this would happen back at home, you won't be able to come instantly? And now it makes no sense to change your decision, especially when you are too vulnerable. Think it out with a calm head and decide for yourself."

"Each one of us is dealing with issues. Problems are different, but in some form or the other, they will be there, always. It's a law that applies to human beings," Vishesh said.

The only motive of talking too much practicality to Pujeet was simple – to not let any feeling of guilt reside within him. It kills and consumes exactly like a parasite does to a log of wood. And the person spends their entire life blaming themselves, voluntarily stepping back from everything good they deserve to be a part of. Otherwise, of the supreme logic that we spoke of to calm Pujeet down, we could seldom apply it to our own selves. We were young, raw and really emotional, brilliant only at giving advice and basically poor at applying it when it came to us.

My friends left for their place after an hour of the whole video interaction. We stood at the gate for some time and talked of planning to visit Pujeet's family at the earliest to pay condolences. In between, Vishesh annoyed both me and Jaffy as he kept going inside, using my bathroom to wash his hands. If I can recall correctly, in sixty minutes, he must have done it nearly ten times, if not more. In our ignorance, we laughed our guts out at him, and he, mildly smiled at our jokes, embarrassed. Failing to control his dire compulsion to do so over and over, he kept going in, trying his best to divert our attention towards something or the other.

An already demolished young man dealing with a broken dream, a shattered heart, a job demanding traits against the nub of his basic nature, and most importantly, a mental state unknown to him and us, would certainly have begun to demolish his confidence and self-esteem.

BOTH VISHESH'S PARENTS ENTERED HIS ROOM AS HE CHANGED clothes. This time, surprisingly, not to present another personal expectation of theirs or to remind him of a duty which they expected their son to fulfil for them with immediate effect. Instead, they came wearing a smile, telling him in unison, that they wanted to gift him something.

"Son, I was thinking that all my friends' kids go to office in a car, so I should buy you one as well." His father had an arm over his mother's shoulder the whole time.

"I mean, why should our boy travel on a bike when we can afford to get him a four wheeler? Don't you think so?" he further added.

"You want to buy me a car because you don't want your friends to feel that your son is riding a bike due to your inability, or his salary is not good enough in comparison to their children?" Vishesh asked with shock clearly plastered on his face.

"What is that supposed to mean?" his mother replied, miffed. "This is more for your safety. Two wheelers are unsafe these days."

"Of course, bikes aren't safe anymore." His father elaborated, "These days the newspapers are filled with news of accidents, majority of which involve bikes."

"Which car do you plan to buy me?" Vishesh asked.

"Any that you like. The budget is four lakhs," his father answered with a grin. "In fact, you can do your research for the latest models in the market and let me know. We will get it next week itself. No delay, I promise."

"I am not fond of cars. I am happy with whatever I have," Vishesh answered.

"Come on, son! If not for you, then for whom will we spend money? It's all yours," his mother said.

"Can you do me a favour, please? What if, in place of buying me a car, you lend me one lakh rupees which I shall slowly return to you in six months?"

"And why do you need the money?" his father asked with suspicion, beneath which he had a clear idea of the answer he was going to get.

"Well, uh…It can help me to…you know, uh…get my… book published."

"Vishesh, I am talking of an asset creation and not throwing money into sewerage. Why can't you get rid of this bug of being a writer? It's time we settle you down with a decent girl and you are thinking of walking on the evil path of destruction."

"I don't think I am ready for marriage," Vishesh declared.

"Then when will you be ready? When all your hair fall off and you have no more teeth left in your mouth? Is that when you plan to start a family?" His mother was annoyed.

"I don't know all that, but this surely isn't the right time," Vishesh said.

"Why not? You have started to earn now. Your mother and I are government employees, plus the girl we find for you will be working too, so where is the problem? Everything is well in place, with the future of everyone totally secure."

"Papa, I respect the fact that I have no right to waste your money because it's the outcome of your sweat, but I think I can take the plunge with mine. The money I earn, I plan to spend it on self-publishing."

"What the hell is wrong with you? Why do you need to waste and learn, and not learn and avoid wastage?" his mother shouted.

"You will hand over to your mother fifteen thousand from your salary for rent, food and electricity. This is how you will learn the value of money, not otherwise," his father declared.

"What? I don't mind giving money to Mom, but why in the name of charges?"

"So that if not you, then at least I can save your money from getting wasted," his father replied.

"What if I refuse?" Vishesh said.

"I swear, you will have to live as a paying guest somewhere else," his mother said.

"What is my fault? Why am I being punished for no mistake of mine? Just because I couldn't get into your desired institute, does it withdraw my right to dream and to try and live it? Tell me?"

"No discussion on your emotional drama. If you want a car, let me know by tomorrow evening…if not, your wish," his father said. "And be very clear about this, I cannot let you have a lengthy silver beard and a cloth bag hanging over your shoulder. That's not the way you are going to live."

"Do writers walk around like hippies? Which century are you living in?"

"Don't teach your father, okay? Ten years down the line, you will thank me for stopping you from having taken this idiotic path. Wait and watch. Let's get out of here Ritu, before he starts weeping like a baby."

And as they left the room, Vishesh controlled himself from slamming his hand on the wall, feeling bitterly bereft. He then ran into the washroom, leaving all the taps open to prevent the sound of his cries from reaching out. For the next few minutes, he stood with his gaze fixed on the water, his fists closed and throat burning to shout out. But instead, he gained control of himself, thinking that it wasn't the right thing to do and closed the taps. Before he could leave the washroom, he stepped back, washed his hands and then returned.

Several hours later, in the dark corner of his room, when he could think of nothing, he tried writing to get some peace. It didn't work out for him this time as his mind was overflowing with emotions. Unable to focus and write down neat sentences even after die-hard repeated attempts, Vishesh picked up his laptop and was almost tempted to smash it on the floor, groaning.

Hours later, when his resentment got the better of him and he needed someone to talk to, he spoke to himself.

"I see you people applauding contestants on music shows. You feel great for kids who fight through adversity and win dance competitions at such a tender age. You encourage me to watch life stories of people who have made it big, those rags to riches stories that appear on talk shows. But I don't understand a simple thing, Papa. Why don't you approve of the only thing I ever asked for? Is following the truth of my inner voice such a disgraceful act? Is it a path that will lead your child nowhere? You remember, you taught me to be a great human being always. Does my dream stop me from being one? Tell me Papa, does it? No! Then why don't you let me be? What's my fault? Let me know, please."

With the given mental state, and beginning of depression getting coupled with it, which again no one knew about, he needed to be doing what he loved. However, people who could help were looking out for security and stability for him, forgetting they had a rare child to whom these things didn't matter. They were basically trying to adjust him into a frame that he wasn't suited for, and that they still, no matter how and in what shape it fit, were bent on pushing him inside.

Soaked in tears, he had fallen asleep finding it hard to realise it was the end of the road and that he should accept the life imposed on him as every path he was trying to desperately think of making, had broken down as well. We would give him hope saying he was too young to feel disheartened and his time would come. To that he'd answer, "If you chop off a bird's wings and ask it to be patient and not howl around, saying they will grow back and it could start flying again soon, do you think it will work? Will the cats, dogs and all other predators let it live? Will they? They won't, because it's at a place it's not meant to be. Also, don't start stating any example anywhere you feel is right. One medicine does not suit every person's body. Alright?"

It was a waste of time debating with him. His answers were always of deeper understanding of achieving gratification than a tool to flash impressive practicality. And in pursuit of that, he once again went on to put everything at stake. After giving fifteen thousand out from his salary at home, Vishesh managed to save nine thousand rupees every month. He avoided lunch, any party or outing and simply put it all in the share market, taking a risk to see if there was any change in his fortune.

Alas, all his money reduced to zero within a few seconds of the gamble. The final nail in the coffin turned out to be when he was accused of stealing his mother's gold chain. He received the beating of his life and his laptop was smashed against the wall by his father and many of his diaries were burnt. Finally, the chain was found beneath the cupboard, though his mother didn't admit to have lost it by mistake and said Vishesh had intentionally kept it there.

For me, personally, even if he had stolen it, he wasn't wrong. The overboard attempts of his parents at controlling his life and their unwillingness to even listen to him was invitation to a catastrophe. It seemed they thought they knew better than everyone else.

The frequency of Vishesh washing his hands was increasing, directly meaning that his disorder was beginning to get worse. Also, his inevitable failure at meeting targets in the office was leading to problems. Every morning in that cubicle, he used to be humiliated and then it was the customers over the phone who would go to the extent of abusing and disgracing him for the expected service he wasn't able to provide.

On performance evaluation day, when the Regional Sales Manager turned up, he sent everybody out and it was only Vishesh inside the room, standing in front of him, ready to face the wrath of the man who could only be impressed by big numbers. He flipped through his performance report and threw it angrily on the floor. The sound it created frightened Vishesh and he shivered a little.

"It has been four months since you joined. Now surely the excuse of training cannot come to your rescue. Having said that, what the hell is your problem, boy? Not even a single mutual fund, not one life insurance worth fifty thousand in your name. What have you been doing here? Taking your salary for free? Is that what your plan is?"

He had nothing to say. After all, no one wants to know of the efforts you made, it's the result the world looks for.

"Speak up, asshole! I want an answer from you. Look into my eyes. Speak!"

Vishesh slowly raised his head, frightened and looked at the face of his angry boss.

"I want a reason for such a poor performance. Speak the fuck up, boy! You are not going home today. I am telling you."

"Sir...uh...I tried fixing calls...but people haven't been giving time."

"Take your phone out, right now, and dial any number from the database allotted to you. I want to see how you talk to customers."

"Sir…"

"Take it out, I said."

He put his hands in his pocket, taking the phone out and said, "Sir, the person who handled these customers last, had done a lot of frauds. He tricked a majority of potential customers because of which they don't trust me. If you say so, I shall ask the branch manager to phone them and verify my statement."

"For the first and the very last time, I am telling you, never talk to me about people who have died or those who have left the organisation. You are being paid, the company expects you to do your job. Simple. We deal in only and only results. If you can't get them, you can resign and leave straightaway."

"I am sorry, sir. I'll take care of it."

"Take my word, motherfucker, it is only for the regard I have for your maternal uncle that I am giving you one last chance. This time, if you don't meet the targets, I will personally come here, grab you by the neck and throw you out of the office. Take it in your head that you will be chasing double the targets than what you are normally supposed to."

"Yes sir," he nodded.

"Get out! Send your branch manager inside."

"Yes sir. Sorry sir," Vishesh mumbled and left.

Bhavna, another colleague of Vishesh, came to him, wheeling her chair, ensuring that no one was watching as Vishesh came back to his seat.

"What did the joker say?" she whispered

"He said less and abused more. Is that the culture here?" Vishesh said.

"What did you expect? You're working for Mark Zuckerberg?" Bhavna said with a smile.

"Still… How could he say anything that came into his mouth? Is that how he would talk to his own son as well? I'll write an email to HR regarding this. Swearing is unacceptable."

"Did you not read the job contract carefully before signing? It was clearly mentioned in bold letters: Half of the salary given will be for getting fucked without making any noise."

"Really?" Vishesh asked astonished.

She giggled covering mouth with her hands.

"Stop joking, Bhavna," he said, annoyed. "I am frustrated and you, instead of giving a solution, are joking."

"I am not saying what he did was right. Only understand that we are all slaves here. It would be better for you to accept it. If you cannot understand that though, go home and work for yourself. Become an entrepreneur."

"If it was that easy, who would have come here in the first place?"

"Exactly, that is my point. We know that we aren't that capable. Had it been the other way round, would anyone need to waste his or her life here? So let's accept our impotency and incapability and save the little we have. Let us not mind listening to his nonsense from one ear, assuming he is a lunatic, and throwing it out from the other. Moreover, he visits only once in a month. I am sure you would agree that this much is still bearable when we get days where we can sit free, laugh, do nothing and go home."

Bhavna evidently was the kind of person who cared about her present day and not taking the road less taken. She was happy earning whatever her salary was and could bear anything, considering it to be a part and parcel of the game. However, the argument she gave in favour of accepting mediocrity was not suitable for a guy who had no fear of the outcome. Although Vishesh was being knocked from every direction, both mentally and financially for the last couple of years, he could not be separated from the only thing that gave meaning to his existence.

I could very well see how much he was missing being himself and that he was desperate to find a way out. Even though no one wanted to publish his work, he still didn't give up on his hope and even after coming home tired from office, taking in all the frustration from the customers and operational work, he would still write longhand every night. Seeing his condition, my faith in god sort of wavered in those days. I mean, what else would work in one's favour if not for the level of dedication he had shown. Maybe the universe, especially in his case, wanted to test him to the fullest. That's why, I guess, he could never get any peace. To make things worse, his being ridiculed at home never stopped. Only the reasons had changed.

His father would often mock his job profile, calling him a 'Cheap Salesvaala Agent', intending it to be just a joke. But sometimes parents don't understand the actual mental state of their kids, resulting in making their children lose their self-dignity. It is sometimes due to this that children begin to argue with parents and the gap between them widens. Vishesh never answered back, but he took a measure that was even worse. After getting free from office, he would sit on a bench of the city railway station, where he'd write things on his diary, watch the trains pass by, look at passengers come and go and return home as late as possible. When asked, he lied that he was attending to some last minute office work. It was the best way according to him to find peace for himself.

Also, Vishesh was losing control over his logical mind. On many nights, he would stand in front of the mirror and talk to his reflection, speaking to it as if it was the sort of father he wanted his father to be. After all, there had to be someone to listen to his pain and reply.

"Papa, I will do everything as per your instructions. Please give me one year for my dream, please."

"No son. In fact, take a lifetime to be who you are. Pledge me sincerity and fall as many times as you want. I'll be there to help you stand up again."

"I'll work hard to the point where you will be proud of me, and all the humiliation you had to suffer when I scored zero marks in my tests, I'll make up for them."

"What sort of humiliation, son? It's totally okay to score a zero. You just weren't meant for that, my child. I observed, you did try to improve at it, but if results weren't good, that simply means you weren't made for it."

"I feel confident when I write. I can sketch characters and put them in words in a way I can do no other job."

"I know, my son. You need not say it. All these medals that hang on the wall, these trophies that you have won, surely don't come without any effort."

"Nothing in this world makes me feel as good as you understanding and encouraging me. One sight of you truly supporting me, your immense faith, and the confidence that no matter what the world may think, you shall trust me, relieves me of dark thoughts of the consequences of my efforts, enabling me to focus more on work."

"Son, what am I here for? If I won't support the dreams of my own child, who else will? And it's not my obligation, it's my duty."

"Thank you for understanding me, Papa. Thank you so much."

He stood silent for a minute.

"And Papa, I want to share one more thing with you."

"Say, my child."

"I don't know why I feel like washing my hands again and again. A constant thought that they have become dirty and that germs would enter my body and kill me always leaves me horrified. If anyone happens to touch me, I feel like I must wash that part vigorously because if I don't, I keep feeling very uncomfortable as if I'll catch a chronic disease. What's wrong with me, Papa? I am unable to figure it out. Help me, please. Help me!"

Outside Vishesh's dream world, despite noticing for a thousand times himself, Hari Lal Uncle kept ignoring it, having no ounce of an idea that his son was in deep trouble. Unfortunately, he was so blinded in keeping his social status, celebrating with his friends and wife outside every other night that he had lost track of his common sense.

I cannot forget an incident myself when I had wanted to use Vishesh's washroom one day but he insisted I go to any other one and not his. And when I ran into it pushing him aside, he knocked on the door like crazy, fought with me when I came out and started to clean it, asking me to go home. I was mad at him as I had no idea of his disorder and deteriorating state of mind.

"A friend who cannot let me use his loo, what the hell can I expect from him in life?" I said.

"Remember, when we were in class eight and I had lost my Hindi notebook? I had requested you to lend it to me to get a photocopy and you said no to me. We had the exam the very next day," Vishesh said

"Dude, what the fuck? We were kids at that time. From where has such old crap come in between us? What are you nurturing in your brain, you asshole?"

"You are an asshole. Not me. And when it comes down to you, we were kids, right? Otherwise, it's me who's wrong. It's always me who is the culprit. In the whole wide world ruled by your almighty god, everybody's got sense, except Vishesh Raghav," he almost screamed.

Surely, he was not the boy I knew. There wasn't the twinkle in his eyes which I had always seen. Instead, this time, his eyes carried fear and suspicion which was shocking. He constantly tried to steal his gaze, addressing me, but looking elsewhere. This person was not Vishesh. He was someone else. Someone totally messed up.

"Vishesh... buddy! What's wrong with you?" I said.

"Let me clean everything, I'll see you later," he said.

"I didn't go pissing around, man." I was agitated. "Why are you behaving like this?"

"I've got to go for some important work in a few minutes, so I was anyway about to ask you to leave," Vishesh said.

I gazed at him angrily for a moment, feeling like giving a tight slap across his face. But then, I thought what good would it do to our relation, and I left his house feeling insulted. Reaching outside, I was just about to sit in my car when I paused and reflected on what had just happened. It took me some time to evaluate and learn. I realised that there was something terribly wrong and that he was not okay. What had happened in there was not a result of some influence or frustration. I needed to talk to him. I went inside again and saw he was rubbing and scrubbing the floor very thoroughly with tissue paper. His breathing was abnormally fast, eyes very close to the ground, as if checking that the germs or insects or whatever had died on the floor were thoroughly gone and the floor was clean again.

Tears fell down my eyes seeing the desperate way he went about cleaning. For what fault was my brother suffering?

Through all the years of knowing him, he never had wished for anything except making his father proud. It was the sole mission of his life to make him feel that he truly cared about his happiness and that he was not a worthless son.

At that moment, the days from the past started clearing the picture for me as I realised Vishesh had always yearned for his parents. I mentally slapped myself as to why I had never noticed the helplessness filled in his eyes during all those state, inter-state, national competitions when he used to be the only participant without anybody in the audience to support and cheer for him. Not even one member from his family would turn up. He always wanted his father to come and see him perform. No one ever cared for his victory, as it was never counted as a constructive effort. At times, I remember, he had to lie in order to participate, and for the fear of his father finding out, he would throw his memento and certificate on the road somewhere.

Now, I could not fathom how I could help him. "Should I address my observation to his father?" Honestly, I was scared to face him. Moreover, if I could notice this in such a short timespan, how hadn't his parents seen it till now? More importantly, if I was wrong, it would be such a shame, and then maybe he would tell my father what I had said about his son. Out of fear and apprehension, I did not do anything. I chose to become a mere spectator, more so behaving like an ostrich where I buried my head in the ground, thinking nothing was wrong.

To make life tougher for Vishesh, his uncle reported his performance at work to his father, complaining that it seemed he had been intentionally not doing it and that the continuance of the same behaviour would lead him to being given a pink slip. His father got into a terrible mood as soon as he heard this. That Sunday afternoon, he barged into Vishesh's room screaming in anger. Vishesh was sleeping, buried under a blanket, which his father grabbed and yanked off violently. Vishesh woke up, soaked in fear, unable to understand what had happened all of a sudden.

"Do you want to suck the fucking life out of me, do you?" His voice pierced through the roof.

His mother and sister came running, wondering what was wrong.

"Why are you yelling, Hari? What has he done now?" his mother asked.

"Don't ask me. Ask this bastard you have borne," he replied. "He wants to send me to my death."

"What on earth is wrong with you?" his mother blasted him. "Why can't you spare us? Look at your father's face! It is red like anything. Do you want to give him a heart attack and make me a widow?"

"Until he sees one of us dead, he will not change his ways," his father said.

"Will anyone please tell me what I have done?" Vishesh said, looking at the three of them, about to break down.

"What do you do in your office? You have been put in the red zone and you did not even bother to inform me?"

He cleared the lump in his throat and replied, "I... I am unable to sell products. They wanted me to do it anyway, even if it didn't suit the needs of the customer. How could I do it? They wanted me to lie and cheat people which I can't do."

"Bloody hell! Is that how you are going to survive in this competitive world? Have I sent you out to become a saint and win appreciation awards for honesty or to earn a damn livelihood for yourself?"

"Papa, I can't fool anyone and make them wrongly invest their money where it is full of risk."

"But you are willing to play with my husband's life, aren't you?" his mother growled. "You would rather prefer to be a thorn for us even at this age when children are supposed to be a support for their parents."

"At least *you* people should try to understand me. If I don't find a suitable customer for a certain product, how can I con them blindly?"

"Shame on you! Still finding an excuse to hide your weaknesses. Now when you are incapable of doing even this, you are trying to shield yourself using terms like humanity, and making us feel that we are selfish and low people, and the entire staff of your company, everyone in the industry is wrong, and it's you, the only one, who is on the path of integrity and rest all of us are sinners. Is that so?"

"Please," he begged. "It's not that I didn't try... I did. It's just not working out."

"What the hell works out for you? Name one single fucking thing that can be expected of you?"

Vishesh lowered his eyes, muttering under his breath, "Why are they always after me?"

"I am telling you, boy. Open your ears wide and listen to me. If you lose the job, there are going to be repercussions that you would have never thought of."

Having said that, his father walked out, banging the door in anger. His mother folded her hands, grunting, "For god's sake, please leave our house if you can't change. Please!" and left followed by his sister.

The next day, Vishesh made around three hundred phone calls to successfully sell a premium product and he got lucky, fixing a meeting with this man named Gaurav Atal with regard to two life insurances worth fifteen lakhs each, against his and his wife's names. If Vishesh could close this deal, he was going to be in for huge rewards, rendering his position safe for a year at least.

He asked his colleague Rahul to accompany him for support, to which he declined, asking him to manage on his own, as he had plans to go on a date.

A LEAN MUSCULAR GUY WEARING A SLEEVELESS GYM t-shirt and Puma pyjamas opened the door. He was tall, very fair, with large confident eyes that imprinted a sense of superiority. He authoritatively asked Vishesh to wait on a chair in the garden and not enter inside. He went back bolting the door, returning half an hour later with an elderly man – his father probably.

Vishesh wasn't even offered water or a cup of tea which made him feel bad at how every agent got treated, as if they aren't humans but uneducated and low class people ready for any sort of compromise.

Vishesh took out all the product brochures from his bag and began to explain all the options to choose from. The young fellow cut him short in a while, requesting him to wait as he wanted his wife to participate as well.

"Nishtha…" he loudly called her out, "Hurry up! We then need to leave for Mr Grewal's party."

Hearing the name, Vishesh was flummoxed, and he so badly prayed crossing his fingers in numbness, for her to not be the girl from his past. Alas! The one who came through was none other than his Nishtha, the one who had been everything to Vishesh. She looked divine in a yellow suit, red bangles, dark orange henna on her hands, and a strand of hair that he used to once love tucking behind her ear, gently kissing her forehead. As they exchanged glances, Nishtha's expression changed from a smile to that of sudden shock. Her husband and father-in-law were busy looking at the brochures, so they did not notice. Vishesh stood up wishing her a good evening, trying hard to avoid meeting her eyes. She responded with a gentle nod of the head and stood beside her husband, keeping a hand on his shoulder.

"Can we begin with the explanation now, fellow?" said Gaurav.

Vishesh started off with a fumble, and kept mixing up the USPs of different products and regretting, giving an impression of a novice with not much idea of handling queries. It hardly took five minutes for the Atals to get mad. They stopped him, asking him to leave and come back prepared some other day. He pleaded for a chance to start over again, but they simply got up and walked away. Nishtha stood there watching the disappointment on his face. She could not believe that the guy who had been a champion in college at public speaking, seminars, debates and everything, would mess up so bad.

Vishesh packed everything, stood up and gathering all strength in the world, looked into her eyes, smiling.

"Thank you for your time, ma'am," he said. "Have a wonderful evening ahead."

She nodded her head quietly and still avoided looking at him.

Vishesh walked out of the house and as soon as he reached the road, he couldn't take it anymore, feeling weak and tired, and almost fell on his knees. It was a dream to spend every day of his life with the girl who had now married someone else. She was the desire that lived in his heart. The pain of losing her was something that he never spoke of to anyone, but after seeing her like that, the pain had resurfaced, stronger. There was no one else to be blamed, but himself. In the name of one passion, he had lost everything he could have had, and then in the end, the passion too had left him.

Vishesh was broken, helpless and wretched. He hadn't done much wrong to be ignored, robbed and misconstrued to this extent. Looking up at the sky, counting all those times when he had shown such strong sincerity towards his goals, relationships and everything else that no one ever tried to understand, he spoke, "God, I won't ask for much, only give me a little from here so that I am at least able to look into my eyes again and answer myself."

It rained heavily that night. Vishesh found shelter under a tree, unable to fight his demons. He had cut himself from everyone, switching his phone off, and submerged himself in the memories of the time he had spent with Nishtha. The promises that he had made to her. The times they could imagine no life without them being together. Time had passed so quickly, with people and circumstances changing even quicker. The champion of the stage, who looked invincible to every sort of opponent, had ultimately fallen down.

Even after reaching home way late in the night, he couldn't get rid of the heaviness that weighed on him. He went straight to his room and locked himself and then stood in front of the mirror, watching his reflection

"*Jeena yahan, marna yahan, iske siva jaana kahan...*" He sang first and then looking at himself disappointed, he spoke after long. "Listen, Vishesh. You are not a doctor, okay? Not an engineer either. Therefore, understand, that in this country, anyone who is not qualified up to the level of such professions, will only be entitled to become a servant. No one will love them and everyone will leave them. Plus, their life would do no good for they will constantly keep stirring the peace of mind of their parents, friends and everyone they care for. So, you do one thing, you...die."

And then he began to laugh out loud which then turned to helpless sobs to full blown crying. It came to a point when he had to put his hand over his mouth so that the voices wouldn't go outside and wake the others up.

The following day in office was going to be as he anticipated. It wasn't going to get any good for him. The branch manager had her head in her hands as she couldn't believe Vishesh had lost on insurance worth thirty lakh rupees. She was flabbergasted and warned him to do something about it till lunch, or she would escalate it to the Regional Head and his sacking would be inevitable then.

Vishesh came out mentally prepared to receive his termination letter at the end of the day. However, Rahul refused to let that happen without putting up a fight. Vishesh had given up; he wanted to go. Rahul argued. He insisted for Vishesh to wait for an hour, asking him to attend any visiting customers mapped to him. Rahul did not mention what he was up to. He just left the branch in a jiffy.

Rahul's target this time was an old couple whose only son, who worked in the Army had achieved martyrdom at the border. A few lakhs that they had received as reparation, they wanted to invest in a fund which could fetch them regular income, enabling them to spend the rest of their years smoothly. The thing was that these people weren't educated at all, and could be fooled easily, especially due to the fact that they could never imagine anyone cheating the parents of a boy who gave his life for the nation.

Rahul tricked them into signing the riskiest product of the category, telling them it was being pooled in a Fixed Deposit, where the money would be safe and they'd continue getting an assured return of eight percent. The old couple signed the papers blindly, without any questions. It was only once when the old father folded his hands requesting, "Babu Ji, please don't sell us anything beyond the formalities we can bear. Our health doesn't allow us to visit the bank time and again. They don't listen to us and keep asking us to come tomorrow, day after, next week and so on. Our only child has died serving the nation; we hope you will accede to our request."

Rahul had this talent – or heartlessness, if I can call it that, but he could, like no other, cut off his heart from the brain while making deals. Probably that's what made him a successful salesman. When he reached the office building, he phoned Vishesh and called him out in the parking without letting anyone know.

Vishesh looked and saw him waving his hand in the distance, standing outside a shop having a cigarette.

"Man, what you are up to?" he asked nearing Rahul.

Rahul grinned from the corner of his mouth, breathing smoke out, showing a file case, saying, "Here, I got the solution to end all your troubles."

"What's this?" he asked, taking the file from his hand and reading the papers inside it.

Rahul smiled as Vishesh ran through the papers. It was a ULIP worth a million rupees.

"Write your employee code over, and slam it on the manager's face. Tell her you have it in you," Rahul said, puffing his cigarette.

"This is your effort; you have to take the credit. I am not taking it away from you," Vishesh said.

"Oh! Now this was not something that I was expecting, drama queen," Rahul said, coughing a bit.

"I am not taking it," Vishesh replied, handing it back.

"Dude look, it only takes a minute for me to strip anyone. I will manage thousands like these anytime I need. This is for you to save your job. Moreover, even if I do no sale for the next six months, no one will dare put their hands on me. I have given them enough business already."

Vishesh remained quiet for a moment. All the scenes and images of what would happen back home if he lost his job ran through his head. Getting ridiculed, continuously being disgraced, and the violence – his parents would start all over. And he was too broken to handle it anymore.

"You are a magician, Rahul," Vishesh said, accepting it. "I will forever be grateful for this favour. Thank you."

Rahul winked.

Vishesh remained outside the branch for a couple of hours to give an impression that he was out for some business. In the afternoon, when he returned, he first, as required, reported to the manager of his successful attempt. She was, as expected, overjoyed. Without wasting any time, she quickly punched the transaction into her account and encouraged Vishesh to keep up the good work as he was way more capable than he thought.

Every colleague smiled at Vishesh, congratulating him as he walked to his desk. After office hours, checking if the security guard had locked everything, Rahul and he trudged together to their respective vehicles.

"So, when can I expect a wonderful treat?" Rahul asked on their way.

"It has to be as per your order, my lord," Vishesh replied. "By the way, how could you be so quick with the ULIP? Where did you dig it from?"

And then Rahul shared how through a reference he had come to know about the old couple, and the pain they were going through. And how since they were too emotionally drowned in the tragedy of their lost son, it was easy to fool them.

Vishesh was perturbed as he learned the facts. Initially, for a moment, he thought Rahul was only kidding, but when it was confirmed that this was the truth, Vishesh reacted aggressively. He fought with Rahul that he was a sinner and that he had no right to cheat anyone. Rahul shouted at him to stop acting like a kid. He argued that the old couple was too old to live beyond six-seven odd months and that this was an opportunity for them to take... to shine their careers.

Vishesh rudely brought up the insensitivity and callousness that Rahul exhibited through his deeds. Rahul became crazy, taunting that non-achievers and those written off had no right to argue over morality and that either such losers should go accomplish goals their way, or better watch and accept what happens.

"Your charity is not required. Take it away," Vishesh said, turning to Rahul as he sat on the Activa.

Rahul did not reply and rode away, pushing Vishesh out of his way.

It pissed Vishesh off even more. He told his father everything, explaining how the following day he might end up losing his job. He couldn't bear the fact that innocent people were being cheated.

"What are you feeling guilty about?" his father asked. "Neither have you conned those people, nor did you pitch the product. Why is it hurting you then?"

"Because it was done to save my job. It was done so that I could spend a few more months on a desk I am not fit to sit on," Vishesh said.

"Explain to me in clear words, what are you trying to convey?" his father asked.

"I am sorry, but when I tell the truth tomorrow to the manager, I am surely going to be thrown out for good," Vishesh said.

"You will not do anything of that sort," his father said. "Tape your mouth shut and sit quiet."

"Sit quiet and see how those people will cry a year later when agents will knock on their door asking for the next instalment of the premium due, when instead, they deserve to get interest?"

"The one who cheated them will pay. You've got nothing to do with it," his father said

"I never expected this from you. Never," Vishesh said to his father.

"What did you just say?"

"That I never expected this from you," Vishesh repeated.

"You are saying this to the man who brought you up, who paid your school fee, took you to places he couldn't afford to go, stayed up all night when you used to be sick. Now you will teach me what's good and what's not? Who are you? What is your worth? I cannot listen to anything from a boy who couldn't even get a job on his own."

His father did not stop jeering at him. Meanwhile, with shoulders drooping, Vishesh walked off to his dark room, gently bolting the door. He sat on the bed, keeping his bag aside, and a drop of tear fell from his eye. He could still hear his father grumbling. He got up to wash his hands. It seemed to him that a failure like him had no right even to stand for the truth. It was only and only for the IIT-ians or MBAs from branded institutes, or only people earning lots of money, who could put forward their opinions. Ones like him were meant to be servants, and must always keep their heads down and continuously apologise for being 'unsuccessful'.

He also came face to face with a feeling inside that he had been escaping for a while now, and it was a fact that he simply had no future. He had failed. He had fallen. It was the end of the road and he needed to accept that no magic would ever happen. He was ordinary, not the chosen one like he had thought himself to be. Out of everything he had planned, nothing had materialised and he had only brought misery to his loved ones.

Vishesh got up jolted from his bed. He looked around and it was all dark. It took him a moment to calm down and wait for the sweat on his body to dry up. He realised that it was just a dream. No conversation regarding insurance done unethically had happened with his father or mother. It relaxed him to a certain extent. He fell back with arms spread out. "What was that?" he whispered, "Almost so real."

Vishesh got out of bed, feeling the lack of energy. He filled a glass of water and drank it in one go. Then, he sat on the bed, lighting up the fluorescent bulb. It was 01:30 a.m.

That evening, Vishesh had tried to convey the incident to his parents. But, he would just stop short, thinking of their reaction as he was afraid that it would result in no solution. He was sure that no matter what he said or did to convince them, he would end up on the losing side. If his parents agreed to his telling the truth to the manager, he was sure to be fired. In case they refused to agree, how could he live under the weight of cheating those innocent people?

Vishesh could see his future right in front of his eyes. Another phase of humiliation, disgrace, frustration for his family and him as well.

Having said that, what was Vishesh going to do? What else could now be expected from a person like him? Talk to the mirror like he always did, or scream his frustration out to the pillow, or hope more against hope for a divine intervention to happen, without him making any efforts for months.

Vishesh could not help but worry about the trouble the old couple might get into. It was killing him inside and he had to get himself free from the guilt of being party to it. In fact, free from everything. He had now reached the point where he had lost the last bit of himself as well. The dream had a massive impact on his mind and since he was already in deep trouble due to his mental disorder, he failed to hold himself. An extreme reaction from him, thereby, was just a matter of a little more time.

Vishesh ensured everyone was sleeping, took out a hammer from the store room and then walked to the gate. He cautiously climbed over it, checking if there was anyone around, brought the hood of his jacket over his head and ran. There wasn't any question or confusion in his head. It was sheer numbness that occupied it. He could only listen to the sound of his steps and feel his tears soaking his face. What was he going to do? What'd be the ultimate thing to bring him peace?

Quite clearly, the gravely wide communication gap between Vishesh and his parents had played a big role in this particular situation. The presumed result of the discussion about revealing the truth to his parents was a perception of his mind, based on his past experiences with them. And that was not sure to happen. It could have been an exceptional reaction this time, for all we knew. I mean, who knows, Vishesh's parents would have felt proud of their son as not many on earth can take loss at the cost of truth.

Vishesh broke the lock of the shutter of his office, took the file out from the cabin using the flashlight of his phone, looked at it fixedly, gasping heavily and then going to the pantry, found a matchstick. He noted down the contact number of the old couple in his phone, and then, one by one, he burnt all the papers and the cheque attached, watching it reduce to ashes slowly. And then... he screamed. With all his might. It was as if in one go, he wanted to puke out his entire frustration from the loss of love, of dreams, of hope, of being unheard that had constantly been consuming him.

When he came out of the building, slightly relieved at having done the right thing and not caring to clear the mess, Vishesh typed a message to the contact number he had copied to not sign any further deals with the agent they had met, for he was cheating them.

Then, he typed an email to the three of us:

Dear friends,

I don't have anyone more important than the three of you. Whatever good I was able to accomplish years ago, it was certainly because you were always there to cheer for me. You are all amazing and I'll miss you. Until now, if living was worth it, it was due to the fact that I was getting to see you every day or often. Otherwise I would have done this long ago.

I am going away pals, and I don't think I'd ever return. I want to be on my own, far from everything. Never ever think that I didn't see you worthy enough to be made a part of my troubled mind. Only that I am disappointed and unable to carry the weight of mis-stepping every time. More importantly, I am walking away because I don't want to be a constant source of embarrassment to my family.

Tell Papa, I love him from the core of my heart and I am ashamed I could never fulfil his expectations. I very strongly wish I could be good at maths, and would've traded that any day for all my wasteful skills. Unfortunately, I never got the privilege.

Also, when you guys get married and have kids, which I know you are all desperate to have, for my sake, let those beautiful children follow their heart. Don't let them end up like me. In life, happiness is all that matters; the rest, sooner or later, shall follow.
See you.

Vishesh.

And then, clicking on the send button, cross-checking if it had been delivered, he took his SIM card out, squashed it and reduced it to pieces. He then dropped the phone and the hammer into the nearby gutter.

He stood for a moment, looking at the dark starless sky and the wide empty road that led ahead to somewhere in the world.

Vishesh was in an untold agony that had been building inside him for years, and it was for the first time it had converted into an expression. It no longer made sense, he realised, to try and please everybody. No one cared about the others, not about anything except what they specifically wanted anyway.

The elder world claimed through actions and words that their experience was a hard-earned god's voice and that it was a sin on behalf of their kids to ignore it. The behaviour of his own loved ones had been slowly knocking Vishesh down. The roots of values on which he stood until now had finally gotten weak too; they could not take the weight of his heavy heart anymore. After that night, Vishesh never returned home. He had left forever.

In the morning, when I woke up and grabbed my mobile, I saw seventy-eight missed calls from Pujeet. I called him back and he straightaway asked if I had read the email, checking with me if it was a prank or something. I had no clue what he was talking about. I put the call on hold and checked my mailbox to receive the biggest shock of my life. It was a baffling and confusing letter.

In the first place, I wasn't able to believe what I had just learnt, and then secondly, was Vishesh going to kill himself or was he only going away to some other place? The impression I got from the email was quite suicidal, honestly. I ran to Vishesh's home, trying to call him all the way through. The number was not reachable.

The Raghavs had no idea of anything as well. It was simply the beginning of yet another normal day for them. I showed his father the email when I met him at the gate; he was about to leave for his daily jog. He ran inside, stupefied, and looked through the entire house shouting Vishesh's name. He was nowhere to be found. I searched his room in the meantime. He hadn't left a message for anyone. Clearly, he had been too disappointed to say anything directly to his family.

The Raghavs though, very fearful of Vishesh taking the extreme step, decided to wait for two-three days, expecting him to return. After all, he had not taken a thing from home, and there was no other way of sustaining himself, they were sure. Even his wallet was on the table with all the cards inside and none of the clothes had been taken either. Though all this strengthened our suspicion of him having thought of ending his life, we achingly still hoped for his return and well-being.

Vishesh's sister was crying, his mother cursing her stars, about to faint any moment. My eyes were moist. I went to the corner and wept like a child. My partner in crime, my brother, my best friend, the sweetest thing in all my memories, was all alone somewhere, that too in such a vulnerable state of mind, and I didn't have a clue. Hari Lal Uncle was unable to understand what brought this on. He was quiet, sitting like a lost man, running his hands over each other, regretting his behaviour.

A week passed by, waiting. Though the police was looking into the matter, we also searched every possible place we could think of. Regrettably, there were no signs of Vishesh. Those people – the ridiculous bunch of sick people who had looked down upon him all his life, including his relatives – had jumped in as well. They, instead of helping us out, only added to our frustration.

Those retards, in the name of consoling, would repeatedly remark that it was foolish of Vishesh to have taken such a disastrous step and that he was inefficient to stand in the face of adversity and battle out the complex ties of relationships and destiny.

It was lame of them to behave like that. At times, I felt like punching them in their faces. Who had given them the right to say such things? Was everything perfect back in their homes? Could they simply not sit quietly and stay out of the matter?

They did not know anything about Vishesh, he was more of a stranger to them, and yet they were being selfishly judgmental. The poor boy had his dreams broken. A girl whom he loved for so many years left him alone. His parents were never ready to listen to him, considering him stupid for no apparent reason. At work, he was proving to be a total failure. And on top of everything, he was dealing with an untreated OCD.

OCD! Now this reminds me of a very important thing. A few days later, we, along with Hari Lal Uncle went to the psychiatrist who had diagnosed Vishesh's disorder. Initially, the doctor refused to meet us as he was angry for Uncle's not having paid heed to the seriousness of the matter in the first place. But later, when I blocked his way, folding my hands, pleading to him to listen to the entire story, which I quickly narrated, he agreed out of sympathy.

Hari Lal Uncle could not gather the courage to look into the psychiatrist's eyes. Then, through videos of patients suffering, we were given a proper explanation of the mental disorder Vishesh had been battling all by himself. In the video, we saw a patient coming back and checking an electric plug every twenty minutes to make sure it was turned off. In another one, a patient kept washing his hands until the soap was half of its size as he believed that all germs would die only then. Also, in one case, a girl suffering from OCD was accumulating junk, not letting anyone throw it away.

In short, anyone suffering from OCD seemed to be surviving in hell. Under its influence, one simply remains obsessed with whatever the compulsion be and is not able to get out of it without the required therapy. Moreover, not everyone can be treated and only a few manage to escape its clutches.

Unfavourably, people living with this chronic mental illness are very much prone to contemplating and committing suicide. With that being said, the risk drastically goes up with a person being out of a job, failing at work and facing social isolation. And all these three parameters did somewhere apply to Vishesh. Given the sort of obsession he had, of cleaning his hands repeatedly, it only indicated towards one thing – suicide. Because, for a person who was afraid of catching germs, leaving home and surviving elsewhere on his own, wasn't logically a sensible thing to expect.

At the end of our interaction with the doctor, one thing was pretty obvious – all of us were his culprits. We had failed him. We did not speak of Vishesh's behaviour patterns with each other and never tried to help him out. It was shameful for us to have become selfish and careless when our friend needed us the most.

Hari Lal Uncle would call us every day and ask us about all the unusual things Vishesh would do and pen them down to be able to decipher something. He was under infinite pain of losing his son. I don't remember a day of meeting him when he didn't have tears in his eyes. It was difficult for him to be able to speak at times. I had never seen a man become so weak in all my life. He felt like the murderer of his son, of his dreams and the enthusiasm he had for his passion.

Out of ever-increasing guilt and fear of everyday embarrassment, Hari Lal Uncle and his wife cut themselves off socially. No one had seen them strolling in or out of the house in a long while. And this perhaps didn't happen right away when Vishesh left, but after all the waiting and countless prayers of hope had slipped away. Hari Lal Uncle took premature retirement from office, considering he had nothing left to live for. He wished each day he could do all of it again, with a fresh start, with all his love and with a better understanding of Vishesh's likeness.

We regularly visited their home and earnestly tried our best to help them get out of the pain. But then, how could our mere words of comfort help those parents who had lost their only son? It was obvious though that they had loved

Vishesh immensely. One mistake of ignoring a disease, which perhaps most people in India do not understand due to lack of awareness, had cost them just too much.

I had always felt Vishesh had over-protective parents. Something that I personally believed should really have been avoided. Pretty much because he was an artist who was suffocated by boundaries. Taking risks, exploring and thinking of a world beyond the normal variables, were food and water to his existence.

Once, I dared to ask Uncle the reason of his being so strict. His answer made me feel bad for him, sort of. He told me that in his own childhood, he used to make paper bags out of newspapers and used to go about the shops to sell them. He had no money for education. His mother for the entire life of hers, worked in people's homes sweeping, washing clothes, utensils, while he'd sit outside the gate in the chilly winters waiting for her and often fall sick.

He had risen from those depressing circumstances by virtue of his mother's hard work. Very well did he know what lack of money does to people and how it clobbers them and makes them hate life, resulting in people taking extreme steps at times. He then explained his concern regarding his son's unrealistic dreams, saying that in India, from what he saw, new talent was not given many chances. We could not help but agree with him, because Vishesh had tried giving shape to his dreams, and had seen hurdles at every step. Mostly those related to money, to begin with. If one talked of politics, the future was reserved for kids of the contemporaries. In the movie world, the same formula applied. Genuinely talented people were hardly valued in India.

Further, Vishesh's father told us that he was only trying to save his son and that it wasn't his ego to not let Vishesh follow his passion; it was merely an attempt to not let him see bad times like he had seen. Had Vishesh's passion assured a regular source of decent income, he would never have stopped Vishesh from doing anything he wanted to.

But in the end, he did admit that selfishness for a good life for his son had taken a toll on his common sense. Where things could have been tackled by talking, listening and supporting him, everything had gone haywire.

EVERY TIME MY PHONE RANG, OR A MESSAGE POPPED ON THE screen, or someone rang the door bell, I would hope it to be Vishesh. If not him, then at least a single positive update about him. To my increasing disappointment, it always turned out to be something else. Always!

It was hard to come to terms with reality and it strongly reflected as if he no longer existed. I never deleted his phone number though, hoping that one day, when my phone rang, the screen would flash 'Vishesh Raghav calling'. My parents would sympathise and tell me to try enjoying life and that time would heal my pain. At the same time, I guess, nobody knows how to deal with the sort of wounds which can never be cured. They do seem to disappear at times, but they never really leave. Only that the person who has suffered them stops talking about it, realising no one would ever be able to understand.

I'd miss all of Vishesh's inspiring quotes that he'd post on Facebook every day and also in our group chats. In his dire and ever desperate wait, days turned into weeks and weeks into months, and yet, there was no clue of him.

The police wasn't able to track him down either; nor did we get any information or proof about Vishesh ending his life. Every time a human corpse was found, the Raghavs would have their fingers crossed, hoping it wasn't their child's. It gave us some relief that he must be alive, living somewhere. We definitely could have been wrong, but better live in denial that assured of his presence than bearing the agony of having lost him to death.

Life did not stop there. It, in some way or the other, moved on for everybody. Jaffy and I slowly got occupied in our business, and Pujeet returned from Canada as well. Every evening, we sat along quietly and remembered Vishesh. It was tough to enjoy anything without him. The desperation to hear about him made every passing moment a sort of disappointment. He was being terribly missed. We'd, on some days, visit the empty auditorium in the university where he had performed and would recall those times, sitting in the last row. What an entry he always used to make! It wasn't glorified by the spot light or laser beams, but the confidence he oozed was always a treat for the eyes. It was nature's gift to him. I wished he could perform there on stage forever and I swear I would be his audience for all my life.

Two years and three months later...

THAT SATURDAY NIGHT, THE ENTIRE CITY TUNED IN TO THE first episode of the show *India's Got Talent*. A music band was performing from our very own Chandigarh, and the entire city was watching and cheering as word had spread through ads that someone who was our very own was going to be on national television. It was a moment of pride for all the people from 'The City Beautiful'.

The show was halfway through and then came those six young boys, seemingly in their mid-twenties, with their set-up ready on stage. The anchor stood behind the curtain and wished them luck; the judges and audience welcomed them with a smile and a big round of applause, keen to see their bit. Those fellows quickly introduced themselves, and wasting no more time, were up to their respective instruments.

THE ONE FROM THE STARS

Dear Daddy, you for me forever Czar!
There was a time when I was born a star.
A happy day was when I did you proud,
When you could say you love me aloud!

But the pain you have is due to me,
For I bought you tears and ignominy.
Your sleepless nights and frown on the face
All I could bring you was sheer disgrace.
Dear Daddy, you for me forever Czar!
There was a time when I was born a star.

Each glory and hope you could dream
Crushed inside you like a silent scream
You dreamt of me to bring you fame
Not a laurel did I fetch in any game.
Dear Daddy, you for me forever Czar!
There was a time when I was born a star.

There is hurt, and there lives pain
All my life has gone in vain
For what I am, and could ever be
Meaningless is my spring to thee
All sons are great, those who rise
Not a sun, I am a dark cloud
I wish daddy, I could do you proud.
Dear Daddy, you for me forever Czar!
There was a time when I was born a star.

A standing ovation came their way as they were onto the last stanza, which was a slow repetition of the chorus. All the judges had tears in their eyes, and the people covered by camera were seen getting emotional as well. After all, they too were children to somebody and every child in the world would keep their parents' happiness above any treasure offered.

The judges appreciated those guys, said a yes for the next round. One of the producers sitting in the panel, who was the last to give his comments, added, "With all due respect, the music, the voice, the finesse at instruments, was beyond sensational. But what stood out for me were the lyrics. They were simple, truthful and represent the voice of every child's desire. Quite obviously, they came out direct from the heart and I could feel the pain behind every word written. I mean, this is the potential the future musicians of our country have. Hats off! It's the easiest yes that I have given. Thank you for coming, we look forward to more such soulful performances from you."

Then, as the band turned to leave the scene, the same judge leaned over, pressing the coveted golden buzzer. Instantly, the stage erupted in light, music and glitter, showering the contestants in confetti and earning them a ticket straight to the semi-finals. The band members were overjoyed. They had their mouths covered with their hands and looked at each other amazed, not able to believe what had just happened. They jumped on each other, celebrating. The judge raised his hand, requesting for silence, as he wanted to say something.

"I want to, right now, purchase the rights of your song for the next film that I am producing. I am ready to offer you twenty-five lakh rupees for it, people. What say?"

There was stunned silence for a moment, before the audience went crazy hopping, repeatedly shouting yes!

"Another googly!" I thought. "What a turnaround to their fortunes that was!"

The lead singer took to the mike and said, his voice shivering out of joy and disbelief, "Well, I would consider that a privilege. However, you know, none of us wrote the song. It was… It was… umm… one of my seniors who did. His name is Vishesh Raghav."

"Oh my dear god!" I muttered, standing up from my chair, bewildered. I turned around, picked the remote and quickly raised the volume.

The singer further told everyone, "In the second year of my graduation, while appearing for fall semester exams, we had a seat together, and he shared the lyrics with me back then. I'll have to find him out as we haven't been in touch for years now. It'd be rather unethical to take the credit and decision all by ourselves."

"Wow! I am now even a bigger fan of you all," the judge retorted. "Not only are you fellows great artists, but honest human beings too. I don't think you'd need to find him. He must be watching the show and will come hunting you down. Of course he wants his share of money and fame, doesn't he? Let's meet backstage in a while and I shall share my contact with you."

I picked my phone to call Jaffy, and before I could dial his number, his call came in.

"Did you just watch *IGT*?" he asked.

"I did, man," I said

"No words are coming to my mind. I don't know what to say," Jaffy said

Pujeet was calling me in between. I took him on a conference call.

"Brother, did you just see what happened on TV?"

"We did, Pujji. This is incredible. Unbelievable!" I remarked. I was getting goosebumps.

"Let's run to Hari Lal Uncle," Pujeet said, excited. "Not sure if he'd know it by now."

"Yes, I am coming too," I said, equally excited. "You guys reach his house quickly. I'll see you both there."

Before we could inform his family, they had already got the news through phone calls from their relatives, confirming if it was *their* Vishesh Raghav or some other who had written the song. They didn't officially know as well. It was very much likely to be him only, we knew, but could not claim that. So we helped his family search through all Vishesh's diaries to make sure if it was our friend who had put down those lyrics. We were afraid we would not be able to find anything, as many of his diaries had been burnt. Fortunately though, within an hour or so, we got an answer. Jaffy found the song scribbled on a small jacketed pad, and showed it to everyone.

Hari Lal Uncle folded his hands when he read it and began to weep loudly. He fell in my arms, nodding his head, apologising for having been so insensitive to his son.

"Vishesh, my boy, please come back... please. I am sorry. I beg you, my son. I am sorry. Come back. Don't punish your old man this way for his mistakes. I am sorry, son. I am really very sorry. "

"I used to beat him whenever I found him writing," his mother admitted, breaking down at the same time. "And see, what he used to feel about us. I always compared him with others, humiliating him as if he was my enemy. What had happened to me, god? What had happened? Being a mother, at least I should have supported him. I should have respected him. Why didn't I? Why on earth didn't I? He always used to say, 'Mumma, in all the movies, a mother always supports her son's dreams. Why don't you do the same for me?' I should have stood by him. At least I should have motivated him. Appreciating Agnihotri's son, sometimes Sharma's son, sometimes Verma's son, but never my own son. Never my own son."

"Diksha, get a glass of water for them," I asked Vishesh's sister, who stood beside her mother, rubbing her back, trying to compose her.

The Raghavs had their world shattered. Had Vishesh been trusted, he'd have enjoyed this glorious moment along with his family and friends. But now, he was robbed by fate of everything good that he had earned. It took Vishesh years and years to achieve the feat, and alas! He wasn't there to live it. Imagine how that feeling would have killed everyone who loved him.

Vishesh had acted onto his promise. He had said once, "Papa, give me a chance, and I'll bring tears to your eyes. I'll perform that well."

Maybe he was finally given a chance, and he did make everyone cry.

Soon, we got in touch with the band and they told us they'd been performing all the songs that had been written by Vishesh. We told them of his disappearance which they also announced on stage during the semi-finals. They requested on television on behalf of Hari Lal Uncle that if Vishesh was watching, then to please return as everyone was apologetic for their behaviour back home.

There was still no sign of him, and we, to be honest, were now a hundred percent sure that he was not with us anymore. That he was not coming back. Meanwhile, the band went on to win *IGT* and Vishesh's songs won fame and attention all over the country. Local dailies were flooded with news covering the story of the fallen boy who deserved to live. The Raghavs had now got everything they expected their son to bring. They had got enormous respect, attention, a big cheque, the amount of which exceeded the savings of two generations of their family put together, and everybody in the city started knowing them as the parents of the 'extraordinarily talented young man' whose life could have been very different and much better.

In between all of this, I got an idea. Why not take advantage of the tide and finish what Vishesh had left incomplete? So I got Vishesh's phone number reactivated and then hacked into his email account and got hold of the manuscript that he had written. Changing the title, and writing a fresh introduction of Vishesh, illustrating his story, I began to pitch it again to various publishing houses.

Within a period of three months, responses started to come in. This time, the book which seemed to have no potential earlier, was offered an advance of ten lakhs. Wasn't that hilarious? The content was the same, but just because the marketing experts could see the potential of Vishesh's real life story playing at the emotional strings of readers, bringing huge sales, they competed to grab it at any cost.

I, on the other hand, only had one vision – to make Vishesh's book reach the readers and leave it to those genuine book lovers to decide the quality. The contract, after all research and advices, was to be signed with the second best publishing house of the country. They wanted to imbibe some instances from Vishesh's life into the book, making it more saleable and appealing. I agreed to it. Jaffy and Pujeet did not.

Jaffy reasoned, "Do you want people to purchase Vishesh's book out of sympathy? Do you really believe that this would be victory of the perseverance of and dedication to one's dreams that Vishesh relentlessly fought for?"

"At the end of the day, it's ultimately about reaching genuine readers. We leave it up to them to rate Vishesh's quality as a writer," I said.

"Right, but not by capitalising on this market condition when Vishesh is a household name. I mean, had it not been for media to increase their TRP, which they understandably got in huge numbers by playing his story over and over, would Vishesh be this famous? Tell me? Would anyone know him?"

"People know Vishesh because they loved the sort of songs that he wrote," I replied.

Jaffy questioned, "Can you recall all the lyricists of the tracks you often listen to? Leave all that, just name the person who inked your favourite song. I am sure you won't have the faintest idea."

"Listen guys," Jaffy said. "I can bet if we let things happen the way they are going, this book is going to demolish all records. Also, be very sure, not even the strongest critic would dare say a word against it, as at the end of the day, they'll have to keep public sentiment above the call of duty, choosing to be neutral when it comes to Vishesh's work. So being his true friends, let's not allow this to happen. To make our friend immortal, let's have his work fight like that of an unknown and an ordinary beginner. If it's worthy enough, it will reach its deserved pinnacle. And you know what, we actually get to prove to the world that when nothing went in Vishesh's favour, it was only one bad phase which lasted much longer than it should have. If this book can do well keeping the author's name anonymous, it would, trust me, then acclaim him as a champion."

"So we get this work published with some other name and that's it?" I asked.

"Not at all. This should last till the time the book does well on the basis of its content. Once it is done, and is a hit among people, we will declare the truth," Jaffy said.

Agreeing to Jaffy's point of view, we refused to accept any sort of change. The work had to stay as it was, except for the editorial changes required. Also, the publishers were asked to use a ghost name instead. They did not agree to it initially. When we threatened to withdraw from the contract, they decided to take the plunge on the counter condition of not paying any advance amount. We were happy to accept that.

After a compulsory period of production that every book must pass through, the pre-orders were started on Vishesh's birthday. The homework on marketing front had not been done much. We had no idea how to promote a book. The few strategies we got to know from here and there, we applied; although they were surely not enough to quickly pull things off. Even Vishesh's book's Facebook page that we made had garnered a few hundred likes only. Thus, we knew, the beginning was going to be fairly slow. But as the saying goes: 'When hard work, honest intentions and courage come together, success is inevitable. Yes, it may get delayed for some reasons; it's sure on its way.' So we kept our spirits high.

For the first nine months, the reviews were excellent, yet sales were a matter of concern. It moved at snail's pace, with only twenty/ twenty-five copies selling on an everyday basis. The rankings on different e-commerce portals were a little frustrating to take. We sort of wanted the book to become an overnight sensation. Things don't work that way, we realised.

The book wasn't able to make it into the Top 20 in its category. Regardless of us doing some giveaways and distributing it in schools and colleges, it was taking a hell lot of time. We felt it was better for us to hang up our shoes. Nevertheless, we carried on for the sake of our friend's dedication.

As word of mouth generated steadily, the numbers began to pick up. By the end of two years, the aggregate copies sold were quite impressive. The book had managed to sell fifty thousand copies, earning a national bestseller tag. The email account we had put on the book cover for people, in case they wanted to get in touch with the author Vishal Khosla (which was the ghost name used), was flooded with mails from readers who said how crazily they were in love with the book and were anxiously waiting for the next one.

Reading the emails brought incomparable contentment to us and we knew it would have been blissful for Vishesh to go through all of them! After all, that was what he had lived for! Hari Lal Uncle was teary-eyed to know that his son's work was being loved so much by everyone. Vishesh's mother was proud of him and so was his sister. They couldn't believe they had such a talented boy at their home. The outcome was worth the hard work and sacrifice that my friend had put in.

Not to forget, the time we were waiting for, had now finally come. We decided to reveal to the world about the man behind the book. The same was done on Facebook through a video that Jaffy, Pujeet and I featured in. Overnight, the video went viral. Readers shared it massively, and in the next three months, the book sold half a million copies. Vishesh Raghav, who had been forgotten by the world after that *IGT* season ended, was once again making headlines.

Hari Lal Uncle took a lot of the blame on himself in the interviews he gave to news channels and the print media. He had an important message to convey to many parents. "Always believe in the dreams of your children. When you do that, your children will believe more in themselves. Success at the end of the day is only about self-belief, and not where you come from."

It was too late for him to realise that, but at least he had learnt his lesson. He wanted people to avoid making the mistake he had. Sometimes, some things are accidental. They aren't intended, but still happen. Happily, the new print run of the book had got the name of the author who created it: Vishesh Raghav. With his work, he won many hearts, and I could see how much people craved to read more by him. My friend was finally a superstar. His legacy was going to live on forever.

We were ecstatic beyond measure. The world had proven once again that Vishesh was special. He was a true gift to literature. However... however, in between the celebration of Vishesh's fulfilled dreams, lurked some sad hearts with a few simple questions: Which world did Vishesh go to? Why couldn't he be back? Why could he not get a chance to do it all over again? Why could we not hug him again?

There were no answers, yet every day, we were facing these questions from within.

We were sort of sure that it would be only after death that we would meet Vishesh. But life is far more complex and unpredictable than we understand it to be. Isn't it?

AT A *DHABA* ON THE OUTSKIRTS OF KARSOG – A SMALL TOWN in the lap of the Himalayas approximately seventy miles north of Shimla – the owner who had worked in a slaughter house once, tramped angrily to the entrance and kicked a servant right in the chest. The boy fell down, flying on the rugged slope outside.

"You son of a bitch, if you need to wash your hands every two minutes, get out of my place. No need to work here. A customer is waiting for chapatis and you are wasting time, going to the tap again and again. Is your mother sitting over there with her boyfriend?"

The boy was in pain. He coughed, holding his upper body and felt as if life was leaving him. For a moment it was all dark before his eyes. He breathed anxiously from his mouth, trying to let air inside him.

THE ONE FROM THE STARS

Beyond anyone's knowledge, Vishesh Raghav was alive.

The night when he had left his home, he had walked along the highway for two days, unmindful of what he was doing and where on earth he was going. The only thing he knew was that he was too hurt to ever think of coming back. The idea of living in darkness was easier in comparison to taking the burden of failures and expectations and being misunderstood every day, he felt. Moreover, he could not be a continuous source of burden and tension to his parents anymore.

Lorries stopped for Vishesh on the road that he had taken. Seeing a stranger on foot in a place where no public transport was available, the drivers must have been surprised. Many of them voluntarily stopped and offered to drop Vishesh wherever he wished to go. He would not answer to any of them and would pretend to be lost in thoughts, fumbling, and hence they'd drive away thinking he was a lunatic.

While the others of Vishesh's age were rejoicing in the days of youth, he, on his gloomy way, looked for hand pumps and taps to wash hands. When stuck in the middle of nowhere, out of sudden compulsion, he would steal water bottles from the boxes generally kept outside the shop front. Once or twice, he even got caught red-handed, but luckily, somehow managed to flee, escaping a beating every time.

After a couple of weeks of being on foot, managing to eat whatever he could find and even tying a wet cloth around his stomach to not feel hungry, he did not utter a single word to any person he came across. There was no one in all that while who had heard him say anything beyond a mere 'yes' or a 'no'.

Nonetheless, he was a human being too. A social animal in dire need of someone to speak to or else he would have died out of frustration. Thus, he did what he earlier used to do when lonely around everybody. He talked to himself. He loudly sang into the high sky that he walked under, made funny faces, and even took out those peculiar animal-like sounds to entertain his mind. And if that was not enough, he would converse with the tap water that he'd take in his hands. He would look into it, and wittingly ask of the place it was going to go to. After many minutes of not getting the answer from water, he'd laugh squeakily saying, "You are going inside your daddy's stomach, you fool."

With all that happening, another habit of his had unexpectedly died out. Vishesh did not bother to write again. After leaving the job of a waiter in Himachal Pradesh where he stayed for two months after leaving his home, Vishesh took shelter in a Gurudwara in Patna. He reached there in a train that he randomly got into.

Vishesh had made up his mind that he would stay in Karsog forever as it was one of the most soothing places on earth, but the everyday physical abuses of the Dhaba owner forced him to leave. Fortunately for him, the next home was the safest, where he didn't need to worry about food and water. He worked as a *sevadaar* in the Gurudwara during the day time, and in the night, would leave the room given to him and sit near the *sarovar*.

All sevadaars, as a part of regular exercise, one day, were requested to contribute with original bhajans which Vishesh could have easily done; but he did not. He chose to stay quiet and said he had nothing to offer.

Vishesh didn't feel good and confident about himself anymore. The required faith in his ability had vanished. Only those 'I am good for nothing' ideas occupied his being. He had developed this strong belief that he was inferior to everybody.

To find happiness for himself, he would tune into a 'what-if' scenario, and quite often. "What if he had listened to his father and cleared a government job exam? Nishtha would never have left him. They would have got together then and nothing would have gone wrong. He would have spent time in her arms and life would have been just so perfect!"

Of us, he'd muse on, that we, all his friends, must have somewhere started with the second innings of our lives. And yes, he was nearly right. In all that time, Pujeet, Jaffy and I had gotten married. But it's only us and our god who knew how brutally Vishesh's presence was missed.

When the four of us sat together in our college days, we always used to share our notorious plans about each other's wedding functions, expecting to have some serious fun. It was almost every time that we made these wild guesses as to who among us would get hitched first and then the remaining three being bachelors would bring the sky down dancing like *chhamiya*. Woefully, nothing like that happened. All we ended up with was a learning that we shouldn't expect even the smallest of wishes to come true. You never know what happens next.

While we were trying to come to terms with fate, predominantly assuming Vishesh was no more, he, far from us, was getting on with fate, helping in cooking *langar* to getting up early in the morning and assisting in cleaning the premises of the holy place. His fellow sevadaars always tried asking him about his family and hometown, but he merely responded with a smile and walked away. Even they were sure that something was wrong with his brain. Those fellows chose not to pry into his affairs, leaving him alone.

After staying there for a few months, Vishesh went out for the first time in the evening, wanting a little break from his regular duties. He carried along a cloth bag that was filled with ten bottles of water. It was midnight when he was returning through Mahatma Gandhi Setu (a bridge over the river Ganges connecting Patna in the south to Hajipur in the north of Bihar) when he noticed a girl standing on the edge, almost about to jump off. She wasn't very tall. Her hair was tied, with one strand flying in the wind. From the angle where Vishesh stood, he could see one side of her face, and it was pretty much in distress.

"I think you don't want to do that," Vishesh said as the girl leaned forward.

The girl was clearly startled, looking to her left. "Who are you?" she asked.

"Who am I?" Vishesh said, pondering over it. "Well… I've got no idea myself. Trying to figure that out for many years, to be honest. It's too complicated."

"You sound like you too are here to commit suicide? Is it?"

"I don't think so," Vishesh said, "But… umm… would you mind telling me, why you want to, you know, end your life?"

"Why should I tell *you*? And by the way, who are you to ask? My father?"

"It's alright, madam. I apologise. You can carry on, peacefully. Take care."

Saying that, Vishesh began to walk away. The girl looked at him, shocked at his blunt behaviour. Maybe his not having asked her twice had hurt her ego.

"I loved him and he left me, breaking all his promises…" She spoke loud enough for him to be able to hear. "It pains when someone you love leaves you to never come back."

Vishesh turned back. Looking into her eyes, he said, being overtly theatrical, "This sounds so-so-so-so-so heart breaking, you know. It's the biggest pain in the world, isn't it?"

The girl did not buy his condolences. She got down carefully and got face to face with him.

"Are you trying to make fun of my problem?" She was smart enough to understand sarcasm.

Vishesh did not answer. Nodding his head, disappointed, he started again to mind his way.

"Dude, here is a girl trying to kill herself before your eyes, and you are showing attitude?"

"Listen, before this turns out to be any filmier, do what you are here to do. Goodbye," Vishesh said dramatically.

"Are you not going to convince me that suicide is a bad thing and that it's the most heinous crime in all of human history and I should walk back to my place?" She was taken aback with his reaction.

"Miss, when you left home, did you think you'll meet a Jack from *Titanic*… or some Aakash from *Anjana Anjani* or a male version of Geet from *Jab We Met* whom you were licensed to come across by virtue of considering this step, and thus your life will as a result of the meeting transform in a positive way?"

"Trust me, I had the same thoughts. Goodness gracious! You can guess so well. And you know what! I knew god would send someone to save me. But you are not doing your duty properly. I'll complain to him," she said innocently.

"Don't worry, I am not doing anything. Goodbye."

"Why don't you get this 'goodbye' tattooed on your forehead, young man? Won't it save your energy, as it happens to be the only word you know properly."

"Thank you for the advice, I'll consider that."

"Are you a virgin?" the girl asked.

"Excuse me?"

"Are you a virgin?" she repeated.

"What kind of a question is that?" Vishesh was confused.

"That's a normal thing to ask."

"No, it's not, and what are you planning to do? Troubling every passer-by to kill time?"

"I have got hold of only you since the morning. The rest all are cruising by in cars and trucks. They don't care about me."

"Morning? You have been here since morning? Did no one notice your stupidity?"

"They only do that when you are in a bikini or showing off a part of your body. They are smart people. They understand when it's of use to them," she sounded sad all of a sudden. "So yeah! I have been trying to gather courage to jump off this bridge. Tried it like thousands of times, but whenever I look down, I begin to feel dizzy."

"Go back home, girl."

"You also come naa. Mom and Dad will be so happy to meet you."

"Are you seriously crazy or what?"

"Okay you go, I am committing suicide," said the girl. "Such an irritating and boring man. There is absolutely no use of you."

Without taking the pain to give her an answer, Vishesh resumed his path, and then, as he covered two hundred metres approximately, he heard this loud jolting scream. Literally shivering, he turned back slowly in fear. The girl was standing there, waiting for him to look back, and as Vishesh did, she broke into mad laughter, taking pleasure in the fear on his face.

Vishesh could hear his heart pounding. It felt like the entire energy of his body had become exhausted, leaving a hole inside chest. He fell there on his knees, taking a moment to collect his breath. The girl got worried. Stopping her laughter abruptly, she ran to him, apologising, asking at the same time if he was fine.

"Go away, you..." Vishesh replied in a weak tone.

Then, he got up on his own, releasing a big gasp. He did not look at the girl. He started walking, choosing to leave and completely ignore her. But as he heard her break down into tears, he gazed here and there, irritated, and asked her why on earth she was acting now. "Do you have any other plans in your head to be tested out?" Vishesh asked exasperated.

The girl did not reply and wiped her tears. They did not stop though, and she kept crying.

"What happened? Will you tell me, please? And isn't it me who should be crying? What are you feeling bad about?"

She did not respond, just kept rubbing her eyes.

Vishesh folded his hands. "Ma'am, see, I am running out of patience here, so I beg you to please tell me why you are crying, or else, I am walking away."

"Go. Just leave. Who is asking you to stay? When the man I loved, he did not, why should a stranger like you? Let me die here! And listen, I didn't mean to hurt you. It's been a long time since I have been happy, so I was only trying to relive the feeling."

"Do your parents love you?"

"What?"

"Do your parents love you?"

"What kind of a question is that?"

"A better one than knowing about my virginity, trust me."

"Of course they do."

"Do they support you in doing what you truly desire to be?"

"Yes, they have always been by my side."

"Are you blind in one eye?"

"Can't you see that I can see? I have got these two big beautiful eyes. Boys fall for me after seeing them."

"You are wearing an artificial limb, are you?"

"Is this some kind of a rapid fire round going on? Hey, are you trying to make me feel like I am in *Koffee with Karan*, because if that is so, you are terrible at it, trust me."

"Your right leg and left hand seem unreal to me. Bring it here, can I touch it?"

"Dude, I am absolutely fine. Are you going nuts?"

"Any mental disorder then?"

"I am absolutely fine. Don't you get that?"

"If all that you say is the truth, then, what else are you looking for? Tell me. What else do you want when you have the most powerful tool to win the world? Though yes, I can well understand how it feels to be left by someone in the middle of all expectations, dreams and a life you are desperately waiting to live with that person. But once they decide to go, you can't grab them by the neck and bring them back. Sadly, they haven't left to return. Now, it'd be wrong on your part to ditch your parents for such a reason. More so, when they support your goals. I am sure you would agree that the only thing that belongs to us is our ambitions, because they never leave us. Follow them, and trust me, you will be stronger than ever before."

"Seems like you have had a broken heart too," she said thoughtfully, with a serene smile on her face now.

"Each one of us has! Just that the reasons are different."

"Hmm... you are right," she said. "But, I gave everything to this guy. Lived like he said and never said no to him for anything ever."

"Will you take one piece of advice from me?" Vishesh asked, without letting her go on and on.

"What kind of advice?"

"The level of dedication you gave to that guy, give it to your inner calling."

"Will it help forget his memories? The promises that he made?"

"Of course, it works like an antidote, and that too without any side effects."

"It's easier said than done dude."

"What we fear more than failing is how our loved ones will look at us when we fail. The moment we know they'll not be bothered by a negative result, we begin to feel good about everything and the pain itself begins to subside," Vishesh explained.

"Wow! You are an impressive philosopher, aren't you?" she said, playing with her hair, really impressed. "You seem to have good experience of convincing people. Otherwise how can you be so sure!"

"We all have at least one life lesson that we can give to the world. This one is my bit."

"Sounds very true though. Thank you. I'll definitely try implementing the teachings from the leaf out of your book. And yes, if it takes you more than twelve hours to try and still not succeed at dying, living is most certainly worth it."

"Rightly said!"

"What's your name by the way, and listen no, don't get me wrong, can I... have your number? Please?" The girl said the last part with a guileless innocence.

Vishesh smirked, looking down. And then there was a brief silence for a minute.

"I hope you will be safe and won't return with the same intent here. Take care of yourself," he replied in a cold listless tone, taking a step back, looking deep into her eyes. "And guess what, next time when you stand on the edge of something, I'm sure it will be happiness and you will dive into it without much thought."

"But…"

And Vishesh, feeling no need to carry the confabulation any further, faded into the distance.

Truly said, one broken heart can only be mended by the words and presence of another broken heart. The girl was lucky to have found Vishesh, but my friend wasn't fortunate to find anyone in his journey to whom he could pour his heart out. It wouldn't also be wrong here to understand that his mental condition had reached a stage where he could not trust anyone with his feelings, thus keeping everything inside of him.

When we are hurt, we are subconsciously looking for someone we can speak to about everything. And if we are choosing not to do so, either we are too mature, or too broken to hope anymore.

The next day, he, along with a sevadaar named Gurcharan Singh was on a scooter, going to Muzzafarpur for Gurudwara Committee's official work. They came across a car that had met with an accident, and the passengers inside were yelling for help. Gurcharan Singh stopped the scooter on the side and ran towards the car to help them. He came to know that two hours had passed since the mishap had taken place, but nobody had stopped to help. The car was going at a high speed and the tyre burst. Skidding and tossing, the car had fallen upside down in the roadside bushes.

Gurcharan called out to Vishesh for help, but Vishesh tried to stop someone else as he was fearful of the blood that he could see inside the car. The OCD created an anxiety wherein he felt that the blood may be contaminated with a chronic virus and if he touched it, it might get inside his body, killing him. It was the toughest war that he was fighting with his mind. Vishesh shouted, pleaded, cried and did everything to make some passing vehicle stop. Not a single person paid heed.

Gurcharan Singh had been calling out to him to come and help. He was unable on his own to pull the people out from the toppled over car. Vishesh shouted loudest into the sky, crying over his helplessness and impotency. He picked a brick from the side and smashed it on the road in anger.

"Fuck you, my mind... fucking kill youuuuuu!" Vishesh screeched.

"They will die, Vishesh!" Gurcharan again shouted at him. "Don't be mean. Nothing will happen to you. Nothing, I promise. Come, please."

He looked at the car. "Help them, Vishesh. You can do it," his conscience said to him. "Your death will not make any difference; theirs will. Help them."

Vishesh almost had his eyes half closed while pulling them out and would dare not look at his hands. Though he instantly wanted to run and wash them, he cut off his brain from all sensations of his body. Vishesh and Gurcharan rescued five people, all part of the same family. They were bleeding profusely and were seriously injured.

Gurcharan slipped his hands inside the pocket of the man who was in the driving seat and took his phone out. He called an ambulance, which arrived within fifteen minutes. Meanwhile, Vishesh disappeared, seeing that his part was done. Gurcharan stopped him, stunned at his behaviour. Vishesh was too overtaken by his anxiety to listen to anyone. He sprinted miles to finally enter a farm and rushed to a tube well where he washed his hands quickly and got half wet. The greasy feeling on his hands and arms was filling him with a sense of revulsion and fear. He was shivering miserably while cleaning himself. Not because of the weather, but his mental ailment.

After he was convinced that he had cleaned himself up properly, he came back to the main road. There, under a tree, he saw a bald man sitting in his underwear, with legs folded and chandan rubbed all over his forehead. He seemed less of a man and more of a polar bear. His entire body, except for his neatly shaven face and head, was covered with thick white hair.

"Young boy, come here!" shouted the man.

Initially, Vishesh was hesitant of going closer. But then he called him chanting Lord Shiva's name and said that he was not going to harm him. He also said that he had been doing penance since many years there. Vishesh finally gathered courage and went up to him.

"Sit down near me, child of some great mother," he said

"Thank you, Guruji. But I am okay standing," Vishesh said, folding his hands.

"Never say no to a saint; it's an insult to him," the saint said.

"Yes, Guruji. I am sorry," Vishesh said, sitting down immediately.

"For how much are you going to sell this field to me?"

"Sell you what, Guruji?"

"This field, my child. This field in front of me. For how much will you sell it to me?" the saint asked.

"I am sorry, Guruji. This is not my land. I don't own it."

"Sure... sure," the saint said. "Even I don't have money to buy it. I was asking out of curiosity."

"Curiosity, Guruji?"

"Yes, I was a property dealer in my young days. But the bug never leaves, you know. Remaining in touch with one's former profession feels good."

"That was a well-paying business. Why did you leave that and become a saint?"

"Because, my boy, this is a better business."

"Alright, so you got into this to earn money?"

"I was encouraged to join after my wife ran away with her two boyfriends."

"Oh! Guruji, everything is okay, but why are you not wearing clothes? Don't you feel cold?"

"Actually, one crazy man pushed me into a canal. My clothes are over there on the branch, hanging. I am waiting for them to dry."

"Oh! I am very sorry to hear that."

"Why are you sorry? Were you that crazy man, huh? Tell me?"

"No, Guruji. I only mean that this should not have happened."

"It's okay. I think our fraternity is going through a bad phase. Some are being thrown in jail, while some are being pushed into canals. This time will pass, I am sure. As soon as our planets get calm, we will be back. For the next two years, Saturn sits heavy on all of us."

"Guruji, you know astrology also?" Vishesh asked out of curiosity.

"Guruji knows everything." The saint almost got aggressive as if his supreme divinity had been challenged. "This man sitting here is not an ordinary man that you see. I am a divine miraculous soul, the only messenger of god in Kalyug, who can tell you exactly what the future has in store for you."

"Really?" Vishesh muttered.

He stopped and thought for a while, *"Should I ask about my future?"* Apparently, this so-called saint who could not see his wife cheating on him or being pushed into a canal by a random guy was clearly lying about being an expert at astrology and any sane man could make it out. But then what was a much-needed cure for Vishesh at that point? What was that he was looking for? Listening to something positive, maybe. Because that's the thing with being a human being. No matter how dark the times, we always are in search of a ray of hope. Deep inside each one of us, a voice reassures us every day: "My time will surely come, and I'll prove I wasn't worthless."

Vishesh showed his hand, expecting something good to come.

"What is your name? Tell me that first?" the saint said.

"My name is Vishesh, Guruji."

"Wow! What a beautiful name that is! Vishesh! Vishesh! Vishesh!" The saint diligently repeated. "A special boy you are, huh? And that's probably what I can read from your hand as well. You love your parents and you want to make them proud. That's the first thing I can see."

"That's the mission of my life. But then, isn't that what every child wants to do? Please tell me something good. Something that even I don't know."

"You are a boy with extraordinary gifts. Very rich you will become. Very rich."

"More, please. Tell me more," Vishesh requested.

"You will have a very religious wife."

"And?"

"And that's it," he replied letting go of his hand.

"You said you know everything that is going to happen. You have told me three things, and out of it, even if one comes true, you will claim to be a great saint. Fraud you are, I must say."

"Boy, what do you expect from me? That I should say tomorrow sharp at 11:02 a.m. you will take Coca Cola out from your fridge and drink it, putting in three extra-large cubes of ice? Is that what you want?"

"Sir, I don't want anything, and I guess your clothes must have dried. Wear them as soon as possible or else you will fall sick."

"It's good to hear someone speaking to me about taking care of myself," Guruji said with a smile.

"You are not going to begin with melodrama here, are you?" Vishesh asked sceptically.

"Thirty years of not seeing my people. And now, before death may consume me any moment as I am too old and weak, all I crave for more than anything is to have people to talk to."

Vishesh took a deep breath, thinking how he needed the same thing. "I can understand your pain. For me, it has been almost two years now and I miss them all. I know how bad it must be on you with so many decades gone by."

"You also ran away from home?"

"Yes."

"Step mother treats you like you are a punching bag?"

Vishesh smiled at the filmy guess. "Whatever it may be, I like to keep it personal."

"I'll give you advice worth a million rupees, boy." The saint said, "If you are bent on not returning back, become like me. Perhaps a popular version, I would reckon. At least you will easily find people to talk to. Otherwise, trust me, it feels very very lonely. Especially after five or six years, one feels like banging one's head on everything and die. Situations may, in fact, get worse to an extent that you lose all your rationale and mental powers. You have lost half already, I believe. Children will pelt stones at you and everyone who sees you will make fun of you."

"Guruji, are you trying to instil fear in me… with a hidden agenda of trying to convince me to go home, maybe?"

"Son, no one can instil anything in people like you. The insect that has got inside your brain, the one which has forced you to leave your family, nothing can kill its power. It's invincible now. Like AIDS, like last stage cancer. You understand that? Tight slaps from your father could certainly have helped initially, but now, only death will set you free."

The saint was spot on about telling Vishesh of his unwillingness to ever return and that the best of medicines or emphatic counselling sessions could not come to his rescue. Vishesh knew that deep inside, but hearing it from another man broke his heart. It revived all the memories of those good old days. After all, he did miss being at home.

Vishesh quietly strolled back to the Gurudwara. He was opening the lock of his room when Gurcharan came from behind.

"You have done a great job today, you know that?" he said

"I am really sorry," Vishesh said, guilt ridden.

"Sorry? Seriously? Ten minutes you wasted searching for help for them. Were your hands jammed or did you suffer a paralysis attack in your legs? What if someone had died? You are living in Guru Ka Ghar. Do you know what our Gurus did for the society? They got their heads chopped off for all of us. You couldn't even help pull those innocent people out of the car? Shame on you! You don't deserve to live here."

Vishesh reflected for a while. He was feeling guilty for his mistake. "I am ready for any punishment," he replied with tears in his eyes.

"Oye Badshah! Tears in your eyes? What happened?" he came close patting his back, asking sincerely.

"I apologise for such behaviour. I didn't mean that. But I cannot touch everything comfortably. I have to think like thousands of times before doing that. I feel germs will get on my hands and I'll die if I don't get them off. That's why I keep washing them again and again. And then when it was about touching people who were in blood, I lost control over my mind and I messed it up. I am… I am sorry."

"Badshah! You are being mentally weak. Why didn't you tell us about this problem before? But don't you worry now. Take this out from your mind. I'll help you out. By the way, I am going out to get new utensils for langar. They must have reached outside the gate."

"I will come along and help," Vishesh said

"No, it's okay. You are tired. Get some rest."

"I am okay, brother. I will come."

"Alright. As you wish."

All the sevadaars began to unload new utensils and carry them to the kitchen inside the Gurudwara. They carefully transported twenty to thirty *thaals* in one go. The glasses and spoons weren't many and only one person was enough to take care of them. Within fifteen minutes, the task was completed successfully. Then, as the sevadaars were coming back inside, they heard sound of cornets. All of them looked back and saw a handsome tall boy wearing a kurta and jeans with a light pink cloth tied around his waist, gathering a crowd for the *Nukad Natak* or street play, which his team was about to perform.

"Wait a minute! Wait a minute! I'll tell you a story. Wait a minute! I went to an office, they asked for money. I said may I sit, they asked for money. Wait a minute! Wait a minute! Tell me if the same happened to you, wait a minute! Or listen to my story! Wait a minute!"

None of the other sevadaars was interested and they walked their way. Vishesh stopped. He felt as if life had beckoned him once more and the smile on his face suggested the he hadn't been as happy in many years as he was now, at the sight and anticipation for the play to begin. People encircled them in a decent number. A group of people including three girls and two boys jumped out from a Maruti Omni that stood at a distance and people made way for them to enter inside the circle.

As the play went on, Vishesh's happiness increased manifold. The artists would fall flat on the concrete (due to demand of their role) giving their very best, pumping adrenalin into Vishesh's body. It was as if, all of a sudden, he had found the remedy to all his problems. Though not a part of it right now, only Vishesh knew how badly he wanted to join them!

The sequence of joy-giving moments ended as the play wrapped up, bringing Vishesh back to the present state. The artists collected money from people in a black Adidas cap, going around to everyone. Vishesh had nothing to spare for them, and it was time, he realised, to get back and start with Seva work.

Vishesh, for a moment, felt like talking to them and requesting them to include him in their team. But something inside him, like fear of rejection or embarrassment, stopped his feet. Also, since he thought he wasn't capable and efficient of doing it anymore, he chose to stay away. Gazing at their group, expecting, hoping and recalling his own time, he walked back wishing he could still do what had given him so much happiness.

Vishesh was about to enter through the gate of the Gurudwara, when a voice from behind stopped him. It was a girl from the team.

"I have seen you somewhere. I am unable to recollect where," she said, trying to remember.

Vishesh smiled, and replied, "No! I... don't think we have met."

"This voice. This body language... This long beard is creating a little confusion though. I think you are the one who helped me that night."

Vishesh looked at her. He spoke after a while

"That night? Like when... when you were drunk... and had been abandoned in the middle of nowhere, and... three people dropped you home safely? Is that the night you are talking about?" Vishesh said.

"Oh my god! Yes, you are that guy and you remember it! Why didn't you call me then? Where are your friends? How are they?"

"My friends are great. They are doing well. Keep that aside for now. I cannot be happier for you. You are living a wonderful life now. To be an actor and doing street plays, it's just wonderful. I am glad you have found what you were looking for."

"Probably," she answered. "And take this please."

She took out some money from her pocket and handed it over to Vishesh.

"What is this? I cannot take this," Vishesh said.

"At that time, like I said, it was about many people's survival. Now, I have enough money and we are living with respect. Giving this to you would take a weight off my chest, and I believe, if I return your sum, it will be one golden achievement for me. You know, living with a debt makes you feel burdened."

"It wasn't a debt that we gave expecting it to be returned. It was more like helping a friend."

"Listening to these kind words is enough for me. But like I said, if you accept the money, I'll feel I have been able to achieve something. Please don't deprive me of this feeling," the girl said.

Vishesh smiled at her, taking it.

The girl added, "Do say hello to your friends and tell them I am heading back to my native place Kathmandu, and getting married this Sunday. People like you should keep helping more of us. Our faith in god and truth stays intact by virtue of the goodness."

Saying that, she returned to her group, waving her hand.

Truly said, the good you do, someday, in some form, shall surely come back to you.

Thinking of the play and the joy he had received out of hearing about the girl's life, Vishesh began distributing chapatis to the *sangat* at the Gurudwara. To have risen from being a prostitute to being a part of a play group and getting married happily was surely one life to take inspiration from. Though no media would cover that sort of story, for she wasn't an actress or a supermodel or someone who had made it big in Hollywood, she was undoubtedly a champion in her own right.

As Vishesh kept doing his work, many hours later, he realized an important thing. That his anxiety was at its all-time lowest. It was perhaps in a long while that he had not thought of the germs on his hands. He felt like a human being and not a rotten egg after so many years.

"How did it happen?" he thought, stopping in between work, looking carefully at his hands, searching for an answer in flashback.

Was staying away from his passion the biggest mistake that he had committed? Should he have not done anything other than chasing his goal and not given up? His existence was suddenly itching and forcing him to get back to doing what he loved the most. Vishesh was feeling butterflies in his belly and he had to do something about it now. There was this dire urge from within to find a way to do all of it again. Vishesh knew what he had seen in the morning; he could do it better, if not in the best way. The echoes of the claps for the group that had enacted the play outside the Gurudwara were ringing louder and louder in his ears. The Vishesh who used to perform and the magic he'd create was coming before his eyes again and again. He needed to write. He needed to perform. He needed to get back performing his dharma as it was enough of taking obligation of the holy place where he was sowing nothing good for anybody.

After eighteen long months of having left his home, he got rid of the beard for the first time. And then the very next morning, Vishesh left everything behind and took a bus to Kathmandu. Call this Vishesh's nature of being rash or a sudden mad and incomprehensible behaviour of his, he had decided that he would try and find the girl and request her to make him a part of their group. She had told him that she was getting married on Sunday and he was going to search her out. He knew very well that it was going to be next to impossible to find her in such a big city, but he had not a thing to lose.

After a demanding journey of twelve long hours, Vishesh reached his destination. The traditional city exuded a unique atmosphere. The air had a certain divinity that could brighten up a dead person's soul. Vishesh was experiencing a mind-rejuvenating experience and his spirits were high as he was going to be chasing happiness again.

Upon getting down form the bus, the first thing Vishesh did was visit the Pashupatinath Temple about which he had heard quite a bit from his father. It is considered as one of the most important places of worship for Hindu devotees. In the main temple, Vishesh folded his hands, tears slowly dropping down his cheeks. He touched his forehead before the Shivling, requesting god to show him light.

The next day, Vishesh went seeing all the decorated Pashupatinath buildings, and being mesmerised and getting acquainted with the astonishing culture of the place. People around him had both Mongolian as well as Indian features, which felt like he was in some auspicious part of his very own country. Vishesh then made sure to enquire from a few shopkeepers about all the residential areas where he could possibly find the girl. He, for two days, continuously searched for her. But to no avail. The same thing he did on Sunday too, which was supposed to be the day of her wedding, taking the help of a cab driver. However, this time too, he had no luck at all.

Furthermore, the money he had was fast depleting, as being a tourist, he had to pay more than the otherwise normal rates.

"What should I do now?" he thought, looking at the last four notes of hundred rupees each. It was evening time and the sun had gone down, ending his hopes of finding the girl. Walking through the market to the minuscule hotel where he stayed, he saw a placard at the door that read: ***In need of a person. Salary 8000.***

For a minute, he thought of taking it up; then decided against it, rubbishing the thought, making his mind to go back to Patna. Before his departure the next day, Vishesh once again went to the Pashupatinath Temple. This time, he also visited the place where cremations were held, all through the day and night. Vishesh stood there, watching people crying over their loved ones, whose bodies were either on fire or were about to be set on fire. It is believed that no matter how many sins you have done in this life, if your body is cremated in the premises of the holy temple, you go straight to heaven.

After an hour of observing people, he went and sat on the banks of river Bagmati. Vishesh hadn't figured it out, but there was a learned sadhu dressed in saffron with a fairly long *rudraksha mala* around his neck, who had been noticing him.

The sadhu came and sat next to Vishesh, keeping his copper water pot aside and then straightaway asked him about the turmoil Vishesh was in. My friend kept it short, replying that he wasn't able to get any solution to the problems of his life.

The sadhu smiled to it and said, "The biggest problem with human beings is that they don't accept problems as a part of life . They don't try and learn to be happy dealing with them along with everything they have, but would rather spend their entire life running from their share of pain, trying their best to hide from it, forgetting that pain will keep reappearing as it is unavoidable like day and night."

Vishesh nodded. "My story and problems are significantly different. They are nowhere close to what you think."

"Whatever it may be, the solution is the same," the sadhu said.

"And if you don't mind, may I know what that is?" Vishesh asked.

"My job is not to give it to people. No! It is to help them find it out. So better stand up and look inside the river. You will get the answer yourself."

Vishesh had confidence in his words as they were just so emphatically said. He instantly followed the advice. After five minutes of constantly looking at the running water, he turned back and said to the sadhu, "Its only water that I can see, and perhaps two or three types of fish. Where is the thing I am looking for?"

"Spend five more minutes," the sadhu said. "I am sure you will get it."

Vishesh did it uninterrupted for a long time. "I don't think I am getting it," he muttered to himself, irritated and went back and sat down.

"I am glad that you have patience, but sadly, not enough intelligence or faith," the sadhu said.

"I looked carefully. There is nothing, believe me. Maybe it's beginning to get dark, that's why," Vishesh said.

"Stand up. I'll show it to you within a second."

Both of them stood looking into the river.

"Now tell me what you see," the Sadhu asked, holding Vishesh by his arm.

"Water. But no fish this time," was Vishesh's answer

"Look closely. Be more careful. Tell me what you see," the Sadhu forced him again.

"Nothing."

"Don't you see yourself?"

"Me?"

"Yes, you?"

"Wha..?"

"You, my son, you! Don't you have faith in yourself? Don't you count yourself capable enough to do all miracles that you are expecting god to do on your behalf? Was giving you two hands, two legs, and power to think any less, that still the almighty has to intervene to save you or send someone to make you realise your infinite powers?" the sadhu said lovingly.

A brief silence followed.

"You are the best solution to all your problems. Have faith, have confidence in yourself and it'll be done. It's all you need."

"Sadhu ji, see, I am disappointed because I came here to find a group of people who perform street plays. How can I be a solution to find them? Do I build a human tracking system in my body?" Vishesh asked exasperated, not able to figure a way out of his immediate problem.

"Hah! When the ultimate objective is doing street plays, which I assume gives you a lot of, what you call, satisfaction, why do you bank on a team? Can't you do it by yourself? I mean, if I was you, I would have certainly tried it by myself."

Sadhu ji vanished then, giving this last bit of advice. Vishesh remained still, sitting and pondering. *"What this man said was actually practically possible,"* he thought. When on stage, he could perform the role of a lady, eunuch, and even an animal, then why could he not bring everything along in one performance?

Out of the little money he had left, he purchased a book of plays written by Munshi Premchand from a small store. Then, he talked to the hotel owner where he stayed, who was a fragile old man, to employ him as receptionist. The owner after a brief discussion with his wife, agreed to hire him for eight-and-a-half thousand rupees, along with giving permission to sleep under the reception desk and two meals with a strict condition that no hike would be given for at least two years. Vishesh was more than happy to accept the terms without much negotiation.

Vishesh befriended a sixteen-year-old boy named Abhi Chandra, who worked as a housekeeper, waiter, as a help to the chef, and would do everything that any guest would require. Also, he made a deal with Vishesh, whom he used to call bhaiya, that for twenty rupees every day, he would take care of all tasks that Vishesh was supposed to do, as for three to four hours during the evening, Vishesh, sometime in the near future, would need to go to the streets and perform.

Two months went by. Vishesh had started to write. Also, he had learnt by heart all the dialogues from plays in the book. Furthermore, Vishesh had begun to use doctor gloves, which he would never take off, as that made him feel that germs would stay at bay and he wouldn't need to wash hands repeatedly. Strangely, he got the idea of using them when he saw the doctor applying stitches on Abhi Chandra's face when he had once fallen down from the stairs.

Illusion or blasphemy or call it whatever, wearing of gloves saved a lot of his mental energy. Not that it was the end of his OCD, but the number of times he had to wash hands had come down considerably. By virtue of it, Vishesh had grown a lot in confidence as well. He felt from inside that he was getting fine, and slowly this positivity prepared him to ultimately perform before people.

For that, he bought a maroon kurta and a tambourine to begin with. And then, on one fine day, during a late May evening, he finally set out to perform. Vishesh was nervous and was a bit sceptical if he would be able to match the standard he had once set for himself. After all, it was years later that he was going to be doing what he thought he might have lost mastery over.

Vishesh reached Durbar Square in front of the old royal palace of Kathmandu. It is a world heritage site where thousands of tourists continuously pour in to learn about the rich history that is reflected by its intricate wood carvings and beautiful temples and museums.

Vishesh went and stood outside the Kumari Ghar temple, beating the tambourine. People who were entering inside stopped and began to collect around him, and as Vishesh saw a decent rush, he, with all the energy and sense of character, started with the first dialogue.

Instantly, a few people left. Then, as he began the first dialogue of the second character, more left, and then more, and more. Each spectator would hardly stand for a minute and go.

But Vishesh carried on, not letting the disappointment appear on his face. But in ten minutes' time, the only thing every passer-by did was to walk inside the building of the temple, watching him from the corner of their eyes, evidently impressed by his skills, not willing to stop and see his act though.

Maybe most of them, Vishesh thought, didn't understand Hindi. But listening to their words, which they spoke to each other, proved that they knew the language well. It broke his heart. Had his talent and luck faded? Was a single person doing a street play not enough to pull the crowd? Ignoring all these negative ideas, he attempted once again after ten minutes and failed. Gave another break of twenty minutes, tried again, but with the same outcome. Finally, with shoulders drooping, he walked back to work.

The next evening, he gathered courage and went to the same location, beginning to perform at the exact same time. Things started off like they should have, however the result, for some reason or the other, was even worse. People were not attracted. In fact, the average time of each person watching dropped to less than thirty seconds, making Vishesh feel like an embarrassment. It was all funny to think that a person who could blow off sleep of the people in the audience with his fire, was struggling to make a single person watch him. That's time for you!

Nevertheless, he quickly overcame the disappointment and reappeared on the third day, this time at the China Market. Nonetheless, the only good thing happening on this occasion was that he was given a rupee coin by an American couple, presumably because they were kind enough to figure that Vishesh was trying hard. In fact, very hard. It wasn't a joke to carry on till the end with only two people watching, and that too those who clearly did not understand a single word being said.

Three earnest attempts had been total disasters. What was happening? Why was everything going so miserably wrong? He was a man never defeated in plays and debates. At one point of time, it was not only difficult but nearly impossible to match his level of performances. I mean, he had built an aura where every participant would immediately lose hope of winning the first prize, knowing Vishesh Raghav was participating. But what was this? Why was his performance falling apart? How couldn't even a single person be attracted by his work?

Amidst the hopelessness, Vishesh decided to come back stronger with a vengeance. It was natural of him to not give up on performing even when people did not love his bit. And that's one good thing about following your passion, you see. When other things, which have been imposed on us, don't work in our favour, we let them go, easily accepting defeat. But when we see a low in what we super strongly wish to excel in, we work hard and push our limits until we prove a point.

After a gap of seven days, which he used to freshen up his mind, do more of reading dialogues, getting stiffly inside the shoes of characters and a bit of yoga in between to have his focus straight, Vishesh returned. This time though, he was nervous, and that could damage his self-confidence. Unlike the former three times, he did not straightaway start. He held on for a while, his heart beating a little faster than usual, cleared the lump in his throat and began differently – with Hindi couplets that summarized the play. No one bothered to stop and it was done. A much needed spectacular comeback had failed. The caged lion that had expected to come pretty hard, fell flat.

Vishesh did not give a second try. He picked up his handbag up and walked off. During the walk to the hotel, he introspected whether what his father used to say was correct. Maybe he wasn't exceptionally talented and the victories he had in college and university were due to favouritism or something like that. It raised a lot of doubts within him and he almost decided he wouldn't give it another shot. It was for the first time in his life that he wholeheartedly accepted that people like Chetan Bhagat, Amish Tripathi, Ravi Subramanian, Tushar Raheja – these IIT-ians – were entitled to success for they had proven themselves in genuinely judged national level exams.

Vishesh cried, realizing the pain he had caused to his parents, to his love and everybody who cared about his future. He should have listened to them, he regretted. But why had he gone so crazy after a dream that gave him nothing but an exile away from home? Why couldn't he accept a normal life where he'd work for someone, earn a decent sum and give time to all his relationships? Instead, all day, he read that shit in those nonsense motivational books where the authors would beat the trumpet of 'listen to your heart', 'choose your inner calling as a career path', and 'give meaning to your existence'. These words were repeatedly pressed upon him and he would get so influenced that it seemed to be the only right thing for him in the world. Why did he even buy them? Screw all those books and burn them in hell!

He was a failure, he concluded. Losing all his heart, he locked himself in the loo and tightly slapped his own face many times while looking into the mirror, for having caused agony to everybody around him and for being unreasonably adamant on fulfilling his dream. Furthermore, he cursed and abused himself badly for trying all the nonsense again as it brought back the memories that he had been fighting to get over.

"Bhaiya, come out fast. I need to use the loo," Abhi Chandra knocked the door, requesting.

"Coming," Vishesh, said, wiping his face with the sleeves of his kurta.

Lying under the reception desk at around midnight, Vishesh took the play book in his hands, grabbed the pages, and slowly, one by one, reduced them to pieces. Abhi Chandra, who was lying on top of the desk, saw him as he was awake and jumped down asking why he was tearing the book that he so fondly read almost every minute.

"I am actually trying to get rid of an addiction that has spoiled my life. It goes by the name of passion, dreams and what not!" Vishesh answered. "Have treated it like an obsession and loved it like my child. And now, after all that I have sacrificed for it, it has damaged everything that I could be. Moreover, it has not left me any route that can take me back."

"What is your age, bhaiya?"

"My age? Why? You want to find a girl for me?"

"No, not for your marriage. I was only wondering if you are reading this book for exams or just like that. Even I used to tear my books when I wasn't able to understand the chapters. It was so frustrating to study. Not at all enjoyable."

"That means you went to school! I thought you are working here since the day you came into this world."

"I have studied till class eight, bhaiya," he said with some sense of pride.

"At least you should have completed your matric, young brother," Vishesh said.

"Bhaiya, my Papa was a rickshaw-wala. He met with an accident four years back. It was a head on collision with a truck. He was lucky to survive, but now is lying in bed, paralysed. He can't even speak. Have to look after his medicines and, of course, the daily expenditure."

"What about your mother? She too is working?"

"No bhaiya. She cannot. Someone is always needed by Papa's side."

"Oh! I am so sorry to hear that, Abhi."

'Bhaiya, I don't understand one thing..."

"What is that?"

"I can understand my father's condition as to why he can't even try to get up. But there are so many children like me, working in all these hotels, whose fathers, by god's grace, are completely alright and yet most of their kids are doing odd jobs. Had my father been fine, I am sure, I would have been going to school. He would never have let me work like this."

"It's good to hear about the kind of man your father is."

"I am proud of him. Such men deserve to be called heroes. He is my Shaktimaan. Always comes to my rescue. Always."

"You are a child of value, Abhi. You are really a nice chap."

"Bhaiya, you know, my father gave his heart, his soul, every inch of his existence for us. There would pass so many days in a row when he had no customers, and yet he would still go in search of them, expecting good things to happen. We used to make fun of him in innocence sometimes. He'd never be angry and would say, you will learn one day, perhaps when it's too late, that to live with the helplessness of trying and failing is way more satisfying than sitting down accepting defeat and doing nothing but regretting, complaining and grumbling. When taking the latter path, you clearly know it is going to take you nowhere. Then why not take the first route and keep hunting? You have everything to gain."

Abhi Chandra's story touched Vishesh's heart.

"It truly makes sense," Vishesh thought. The only important thing for him to lose in any scenario was his life. Either way, today or tomorrow, it was going to be taken away by nature. So when he was already losing it, why was failure bothering and depressing him so much? The beginning of these thoughts gave him a headache and he did not want to think anymore, so he slept.

"Bhaiya?" Abhi said.

"Bhaiya, have you slept?" he repeated to check.

Vishesh was fast asleep, as both physically and mentally, he was too tired and could no longer keep his eyes open. The next morning when he got up, he felt fresh and ready to go. This time, he decided, he was not going to go to any market and perform, but would do it all for himself, for his own damn happiness. That evening, after the day's work, he went to Mirgasthali – a forest behind Pashupatinath Temple where not many people could be seen, except one or two sadhus. Not to forget, the route to Goraknath Temple went through it.

Vishesh stood amongst the trees, closing his eyes, imagining it to be the centre stage he once used to take. He smiled looking at the landscape. It was lush green. Keeping his bag against a trunk, Vishesh started in his trademark poetic manner.

He ran here and there as he switched characters, and sang and danced and performed his heart out for himself. Few deer saw him and so did a few monkeys sitting on the branches of trees. They didn't go away, nor were they bored. They stood watching him doing his bit. When Vishesh's eyes fell on them, he had a smile, assuming them to be his loyal audience. As a result, he grew in confidence and picked the tempo up.

Those two hours of celebrating his existence were the best hours he had spent in a long while. Therefore, Vishesh decided to return every day and perform. The animals would come as well, stand at a distance like on the first day, and watch Vishesh. Whether it was hot, cold, rainy or humid, Vishesh made sure he did not disappoint his spectators.

Slowly and subtly, six years passed in Nepal. Vishesh began to write plays on his own and perform in the same forest every evening. The animals did certainly join in, and so did many sadhus who would clap and cheer for the messages he gave through his work. Vishesh was happy and bravely fighting his OCD as well by getting clinical help. He had found peace and had thus confined himself to this small world and decided to spend the rest of his life performing there.

But then, life had to throw the dice again. It was, as usual, not going to follow Vishesh's plan. One fine evening, when he was returning from the forest, something very strange happened. Vishesh found a piece of paper lying on the dried leaves. A brick was kept on it so that the wind could not blow it away. He picked it up and it read, 'Vishesh, my friend, I love you'.

He shook his head in bewilderment, as he was too shocked to understand anything. He stood up and looked around shouting. "Whose paper is this? Who has kept it here? Tell me please. Whose paper is this?"

He scuttled here and there like a crazy man, desperately searching for some clue. A paper to be found in a forest was surely no coincidence. Vishesh kept shouting, wanting an answer.

I ran out of patience very quickly and could no longer conceal myself.

But before we came face to face, the question is: how did I find him? Who gave me a clue of Vishesh's existence in Nepal? Was there any person from India who informed me of him, or did I see him in some photo or video of which he accidentally happened to be a part of?

You don't know this Somaya, but your mother and I had no child even after so many years of our marriage. So I had taken this vow that when she conceives, I'd go to Pashupatinath bare feet to offer a thanksgiving prayer. After finishing off with the main purpose of my visit, I went about exploring Kathmandu. It was while going to Gorakhnath Temple with my personal guide in Mirgasthali forest that I heard this voice. It was more than familiar to my ears. I was completely stunned for a moment and my heart went beating faster. I ran in the direction of the voice, and from a distance, saw a man animatedly speaking dialogues. I prayed to god for it to be Vishesh. I was getting goosebumps as I waited for the man to turn a bit. Though I was almost sure from the body language that it was him, I did not want to get disappointed, so I waited. Then, as he turned a little to his right, performing, I was able to see half of his face. My joy knew no bounds. Tears fell from my eyes and I was unable to decipher how to react. I simply could not believe that my friend was alive. I requested my guide to keep a watch on him and stay in touch with me over the phone. Meanwhile, I hurriedly dug out a pen and paper from my bag and wrote a message for him on it. I then requested my guide to leave and paid him his dues. Eyes still on Vishesh, I wondered how time had changed him. As he finished the play to a mild applause, I left the note and hid behind a tree.

Then like I told, Vishesh found the paper, read what was written on it, searched for a clue and then from behind a tree, I came out and uttered his name. He looked in the direction of the sound, turning back. His face full of anxiety and sweat, and his eyes scanning me. We stood looking at each other, feeling wasted. There were a million emotions that our eyes shared in a matter of those few seconds. He looked so completely different with many strands of grey hair, wrinkles and dark shadows under his eyes.

Vishesh and I walked towards each other. He looked into my eyes and then down, feeling like a thief.

"Brother," I said.

He jumped at me, hugging me tightly, breaking into a pool of tears. I could not resist myself as well. My best friend who I had thought was dead, was with me… alive!

"One mail and that's it, brother?" I said, weeping. "At least you should have thought about us. Were we nothing to you?"

"I am sorry, Dhruv. I am really sorry, my brother. I am really sorry." Vishesh was inconsolable. His grip on my arm showed how much he had missed being with us.

"Every day... every single day I have cried thinking you were dead. And you are here, cold to our emotions."

Vishesh said nothing. He only cried and cried as if trying to convey to me the pain he had been in.

"Let's return home," I said, running my hand in his hair. "Everyone is waiting for you"

"Mumma and Papa will be unhappy again, Dhruv. They will again be in all sorts of pain because of me," he said shaking his head.

"Everything has changed, my dear friend. Your world beckons you."

Vishesh looked down, lost in thought. "They all will humiliate me again. I have never given them a single reason to be happy. Now with me being completely useless, not fit to do any job, they will be ashamed to see me."

"Just come, mate," I said, keeping my hand on his shoulder. "You don't know what you have given them."

"Please, Dhruv. I beg you. They must have moved on and must be happy. My worthlessness will start troubling them all over again," he was almost pleading to be not dragged back.

"Vishesh, you have my word. Everyone back home is seriously proud of you. I have met your parents. I know how they have been living."

"No, Dhruv. They can't have a worse life than I was giving them."

"What if I tell you that your father hasn't been doing well since the day you left home? He falls sick almost every day because he is living under the guilt that he murdered you. What if I inform you that every day in the temple, he pleads to god to let him see you and apologise to you."

Vishesh did not answer, but began weeping quietly again.

"Give him a peaceful death, Vishesh. Please come home. Uncle loves you so much."

Vishesh agreed with a great deal of difficulty, fighting his demons. How emotional that was of him! The very knowledge of his father's state of health coaxed him to forget anything and everything that had happened in the past and make him ready to go back in a jiffy. I held him by his hand and packing everything, we left for our country.

I did not tell Vishesh about what he had managed to achieve. I had a plan to do it in a certain way. Also, I did not inform of his return to anybody. Not even to Jaffy and Pujeet. Vishesh asked me how everyone else was doing back home. It had almost been ten years since he had last seen them. I told him that everyone used to mention him in almost everything that they did.

It was our tenth alumni meet and I had started receiving calls from Jaffy and Pujeet to reach soon as the function had already started. Through messages, they were cursing me to have made the Nepal programme at the wrong time, as a result of which I could not join them, spoiling their fun as well. I was at the Patiala bus stand and had just stepped down from the bus with Vishesh. I lied to both my friends that I was still an hour away. This was done because I had phoned Hari Lal Uncle, requesting him to reach the university campus. He had crossed Rajpura and I needed him to reach before I reached there with Vishesh. To him I had said that there was a very special memorial for Vishesh and he had to be present.

I had also kept Vishesh in the dark about all this. He had no idea what I was arranging. All the calls were made and attended getting down from the bus, whenever it stopped. Vishesh was so overwhelmed and amazed looking out through the window, witnessing the change in places after a decade, that he did not suspect what I was up to.

As I received a confirmation call from Uncle that he had reached the campus, we took a cab. Vishesh asked me why we did not go directly to Chandigarh and what was the need to come to Patiala and then go to the university to top it all. I answered that I had some urgent personal work. Meanwhile, Vishesh was nervous thinking of how his family would react on seeing him. He again and again asked me to be by his side through everything. The cab stopped outside Kala Bhawan in centre of the Punjabi University campus. The parking lot was filled with cars that gave a clear idea to Vishesh that some function was going.

We stepped inside and could hear someone speaking into the mike. Both of us were yet to enter the main hall. Then, from the back gate, I took Vishesh to the back entrance of the stage. I asked him to stand there and come out through the side curtain when I announce his name.

He said no apprehensively. I straightaway left saying that he had to swear on my unborn child that he would come out. Vishesh still had no idea what I was up to or what was going on. I was cleverly giving him no room to think. He could not see that until he lifted the curtain or came out.

Then, as I got on stage, our batch-mate Navjot Kaur was inviting people to play 'Match of The Year". I reached her and asked for the mike. She was surprised seeing me in slippers and a shabby jeans and t-shirt with my hair all messed up, as if I had come straight out of bed. In fact, everyone went quiet on seeing me in such a state. The commotion had all of a sudden stopped.

Navjot passed the mike to me, still wondering.

"I've got something very important to say. First of all, I am really sorry for appearing on stage without requesting to be part of the schedule. But trust me, you are going to love me after this. Today, I want all of you to meet a very special person. In fact, a truly special person. A person who teaches us each day to never quit what we love doing. No matter how hard the journey is, live for the truth, and then no matter how much pain it brings to you, just know you stood for the right cause. An association with him makes me feel proud of myself. Many of us tell our kids about him to inspire them.

He is my best friend, an inspiration, and perhaps one among us, whom we think of every single day. A famous songwriter, an acclaimed novelist who has till date sold more than two million copies... Dear friends, please welcome none other than... Vishesh Raghav!"

Every person in the audience stood up in shock. There was sudden chaos as people talked among themselves. They thought I was cracking a bad joke. Meanwhile, I looked behind and there was no one. Pujeet and Jaffy ran on the stage to me. They were baffled. I waited for a minute, still looking back. "What are you saying?" both of them asked.

My attention was still back stage, to where Vishesh had been standing a while ago. No one walked out. I went to check. Pujeet and Jaffy followed. Vishesh was standing perplexed behind the curtain. Again, that head was down and the eyes bereft of any confidence. I held him by the arm and pulled him onto the stage. Both Jaffy and Pujeet yelled his name and hugged him tight, crying bitterly. The audience was in a state of absolute shock.

Vishesh made no eye contact with anyone. I brought him to the centre. There was pin-drop silence. Everyone was in a state of utter disbelief.

"Take this mike, Vishesh, say something. All your friends want to listen to you again. What you left incomplete is done now. Your book is published, my friend. Not only each one of us got a copy of it, but exactly two million people have purchased it. Your father is proud of you."

Vishesh was still looking down, unable to digest what was happening. It seemed he was perceiving it all of it to be a torturous dream that was meant to tease him.

"Vishesh, take the mike. We want to listen to you again," someone shouted from the audience.

He did not respond.

"Buddy, you have made it. You are the bestselling writer you wanted to be," Jaffy and Pujeet said in unison.

Vishesh looked into our eyes. "But I am not an IIT-ian," he slowly whispered, crying. A boy full of faith once, who could achieve anything perhaps, couldn't trust his own achievements. A clear result of people continuously telling him that he was good for nothing.

The door then suddenly made a squeaking sound through which Hari Lal Uncle entered. He must have heard that phrase. He staggered seeing his son. His phone and handkerchief slipped from his hands. Vishesh saw him too. All of us looked at Vishesh and his father.

Vishesh was in more tears than ever now.

"*Meraaa…. beta,*" Uncle sobbed, rubbing his chest.

Vishesh folded his hands, as if apologising.

Uncle was visibly jolted. Tears rolled down from his eyes too, and he folded his hands and fell on his knees. He was sorry for everything he had said to Vishesh. Our tears flowed down in streams. Our friend, our brother had come back.

Epilogue

"Dad," I say, almost about to weep. "Where is Vishesh Uncle now, and why didn't you ever mention him before? I so want to meet him."

Papa releases a breath, closing his eyes. He replies, "For that, you've got to blame your Mumma, Somaya. When you were seven months, she left me to only return two years back."

"Yes, you blame me for everything, and what about your mother?" Mumma revolts. "That lady used to trouble me like anything. And you were such an insensitive husband that you could not see my pain."

"How can you talk like that about my mother?" Papa almost yells.

"Don't you both start again, please," I almost scream.

A silence follows.

"Papa, tell me where is Vishesh Uncle now."

"He is in America, Somaya. He has been there for the last five years, working as a motivational speaker. He is also a teacher, writer, blogger and what not!"

"But when am I meeting him? I need his autograph," I say.

"He is coming back next month, my child," Papa answers with a grin, showing me their group photo on his phone.

Wow! Incredible for someone to dream and make all those dreams come true. I have so many questions to ask Vishesh Uncle. I look forward to meet him. I am sure it's going to be a great experience.

And no matter what my result is, I know I will never give up and do all it takes to fulfil my dreams.

About the author

Keshav Aneel is a young bestselling author who stepped into the world of books with the love story *Promise Me a Million Times* (2016). The book won accolades for its philosophical writing style and the way relationships were explored at various levels through the story.

Right from his teenage days, Keshav was clear about his passion for writing, and has been an active theatre artist and a playwright since then. Although an MBA by qualification, he decided to follow his heart and go after his goal, choosing his inner calling over the corporate world. He is also a University Gold Medallist in Parliamentary Debate, and has been on national stage thrice.

Not to forget, he has formerly worked as a teacher of Digital Marketing and Economics, and loves interacting with people through this particular medium as well.

In his free time, Keshav travels extensively on his own, as that, he believes, helps in self-discovery. His hobbies include playing cricket and football, and he loves autobiographical books and movies.